DEATH OF A SPY

The Hamish Macbeth series

DEATH OF A SPY

M.C. Beaton

with R.W. Green

GRAND CENTRAL

NEW YORK   BOSTON

Grand Central Publishing
Hachette Book Group
1290 Avenue of the Americas, New York, NY 10104
grandcentralpublishing.com
twitter.com/grandcentralpub

First U.S. Edition: February 2024
Also published in Great Britain by Constable

Grand Central Publishing is a division of Hachette Book Group, Inc. The Grand Central Publishing name and logo is a registered trademark of Hachette Book Group, Inc.

The publisher is not responsible for websites (or their content) that are not owned by the publisher.

The Hachette Speakers Bureau provides a wide range of authors for speaking events. To find out more, go to hachettespeakersbureau.com or email HachetteSpeakers@hbgusa.com.

Grand Central Publishing books may be purchased in bulk for business, educational, or promotional use. For information, please contact your local bookseller or the Hachette Book Group Special Markets Department at special.markets@hbgusa.com.

Library of Congress Cataloging-in-Publication Data has been applied for.

ISBNs: 978-1-5387-4330-0 (hardcover), 978-1-5387-6659-0 (large type), 978-1-5387-4332-4 (ebook)

Printed in the United States of America

LSC-C

Printing 1, 2023

Foreword by R. W. Green

Those of you who know Hamish Macbeth and who know a bit about Lochdubh, the village where he lives in Sutherland, in the far northwest of the Scottish Highlands, will also know what the Lochdubh residents think of their local police officer. He's a lazy, work-shy layabout who'd rather be scrounging cups of coffee at the Tommel Castle Hotel or the Italian restaurant in the village than concentrating on the ever-growing list of important matters with which he should be dealing. How can we all sleep safe in our beds with only this dunderheid standing between us and the hordes of lawless scunners rampaging around the Highlands? Well, that's what some of them think.

But does that sound like the Hamish you know? Why would any of the good folk of Lochdubh have such a low opinion of him? Why brand him as lazy? Basically, that all comes down to the wonderful M. C. Beaton—Marion. When she first created her Highland policeman around forty years ago, Marion decided that he should be an outsider rather than a Lochdubh native. Having lived in Sutherland for a while, but having been born and brought up way down south in Glasgow, Marion knew that making him an outsider would give him a little extra work to do in winning over the people who lived on his patch. She decided, therefore, that he was born outside Sutherland in Cromarty, which is to the southeast, and raised in Rogart, which is in the east of Sutherland, about as far away from the fictional Lochdubh on the west coast as you can get without leaving the county.

Marion also knew that it takes a special kind of fortitude to live and work in a place as remote, and with such an unforgiving climate, as Sutherland. She maintained that Sutherlanders can, justifiably, set themselves apart from the rest of the UK population. They have to work hard and, when that work is outdoors, often in harsh conditions. That leads them to reserve judgment on newcomers until they've seen if they have what it takes—and that could take a lifetime. Whether the interloper has come from London, Edinburgh, Glasgow or closer to home, like Hamish, outsiders can remain outsiders until their dying day.

As an outsider in Lochdubh, Hamish was not only different, but was seen to be doing things differently. His relaxed, laid-back manner rankled with some, and the fact that he lived at the police station in what they saw as a "free" house, as well as driving around in a "free" car, made his attitude seem all the more lackadaisical. From there, Marion was able to instill a little jealousy and even a pinch of resentment toward Hamish among some of the Lochdubh residents.

What they failed to realize, of course, was that being a rural police officer is far more work than it might seem. Unlike UK city cops, who clock off at their station and change out of their uniforms to travel home anonymously (although they're still required to intervene should they come across some kind of incident) to neighborhoods where most of those living nearby will have no idea what they do for a living, police officers in rural areas are almost constantly on duty. Everyone knows who they are, where they live and how to contact them should the need arise. They are a vital part of the local community.

Hamish, therefore, works long hours. He also looks after his pets, Lugs and Sonsie, while also tending to his chickens in their garden shed and a few sheep up on the hillside. Choosing to cope with all that doesn't sound like the behavior of a lazy man, does it? Despite all his hard work, Hamish will never either expect or receive credit for his efforts from some in Lochdubh. They see a public servant as public property paid for from the public purse and, with a healthy dose of Highland thrift, they expect to get their taxpayer money's worth.

Being under-appreciated is not something that troubles Hamish in the slightest. Part of the perception of him being lazy stems from his lack of ambition. He will happily allow others further up the police chain of command to take credit for his efforts as long as he is allowed to continue leading a quiet life in Lochdubh. In the village, he can use guile and a little rule bending to remain in control of his own destiny— the last thing he wants is a promotion that would mean leaving the area he has come to love so much.

That is the Hamish Marion introduced me to. She seemed to know him so well that I had to ask her if he was based on someone she knew—surely he hadn't come entirely from her imagination? She had a little twinkle in her eye when she told me that neither Hamish nor any of the other characters in Lochdubh were created entirely in her own head. As a former journalist, Marion always liked to have the TV news playing somewhere in the background. She watched people on TV and, like all good journalists, she was an excellent observer. She observed people she met, even those simply passing by on the street, and identified different physical attributes, different habits and different personality traits, committing them to memory, drawing on that jumble of mental images when she built a new character.

That's the long-winded analysis. The way she explained it was simply that she remembered bits and pieces about people and used them as and when she needed. I learned a huge amount from Marion and regard it as an enormous honor that she was happy for me to carry her characters forward into new adventures, adding a few new faces here and there when the need arose.

New faces are actually what Sutherland desperately needs. It is a vast area with an enormous coastline and scenery that ranges from beautifully bleak moorland to majestic mountain ranges. In all, it covers over 2,000 square miles yet has a population of only 13,500. Compare that to Greater London, which covers just 607 square miles but has a population of more than 9.6 million. Sutherland also has an aging population. Young people grow up and move away for career opportunities in the big cities, meaning that there are fewer young families in the region every year. Schools in Sutherland operate at 29 percent capacity and the population decline is predicted to continue. That adds to the remoteness of the area. A recent survey defined remoteness by how easy it is for those living in a specific area to access a population center of 10,000 people within thirty minutes. Apart from its far southeastern corner, Sutherland was judged the most remote place in the UK, including the Scottish islands.

At this point, we're in danger of confusing fiction and reality. Marion made Lochdubh seem like a very real place by creating its setting, as she did its population, from bits and pieces of other places around Sutherland. You should go there and see for yourself. If you're like me, you won't be able to avoid the disappointment of not seeing signposts for the fictional Strathbane, Lochdubh or Braikie when you're driving around but there are plenty of other places that you will recognize from Hamish's travels. Poor Hamish is forever caught in a quandary—all he wants is to stay at home in Lochdubh, yet to do so he has to hunt down ne'er-do-wells all over the country!

In *Death of a Spy*, Hamish has to hit the road once again, but only once he's solved the problem of the Anstey Bridge Disaster. I hope you enjoy this visit to Hamish Macbeth country as much as I did!

Rod Green, 2024

CHAPTER ONE

Every man at the bottom of his heart believes that he is a born detective.

John Buchan, *The Power-House*

He watched the headlights sweep through swathes of darkness as he guided the car along the coast road. On this stretch there were no houses for miles around, no streetlights, and tonight the moon wouldn't put in an appearance until well after midnight. To his right the hillside climbed steeply up toward the craggy peaks and chill waters of the many tarns nestled in the crumpled mountain skirts of the 3,000-foot Beinn Bhàn. To his left, the inky waters of the Inner Sound stretched five miles to the island of Raasay, where the hills shielded him from the even more distant lights of Portree on the Isle of Skye.

Tonight, the black night was his friend and the intrusion of his headlights made him feel almost guilty. Disturbing the still silence of the dark was not his intention, but it was a necessary transgression. He knew a spot where he could pull off the road just before Applecross Sands and enjoy an uninterrupted view of the clear, cloudless night sky. Glancing down at the binoculars and small telescope in the passenger footwell, he smiled, wondering how many stars he would be able to identify among the thousands he would see. With no competition from human-made, terrestrial light sources, the sky would be a blaze of stars.

His eyes flicked back to the route ahead and he gasped in alarm. There was a body lying in the road! He slammed on the brakes and the tires bit into the surface for a moment before the frantic drumming of the anti-lock brakes brought the car to a halt. He peered out through the windscreen and could clearly see a man lying a few feet in front, illuminated in his headlight beams. Beyond the fallen man stood another car, a silver Audi, facing him on the narrow, single-track road, its headlights extinguished and the driver's door open wide.

Flinging open his own door, he rushed over to the prostrate figure, oblivious to a momentary flash of bright light from the darkness up on the hill. He crouched beside the body.

"Are you hurt?" he called, looking for injuries. "Can you hear me?"

Then the body moved, the head turning to stare up at him with vaguely familiar, half-remembered eyes.

"What...?" he breathed, then heard a footstep behind him. He turned in time to see a baseball bat chopping through the air toward his head. He tried to dodge but the blow caught him on the neck and he collapsed on the ground. The powerful figure wielding the bat took another swing and knocked him senseless.

The man who had been on the ground was quickly on his feet, rolling the barely conscious driver onto a tarpaulin sheet and dragging him out of the way while the batsman swiftly jumped into his victim's car, maneuvering it to the edge of the road. There, the headlights picked out a short stretch of boulder-strewn scrub that fell away toward the edge of a cliff. Leaving the engine running, he leapt out, sprinting over to the Audi and starting it up. With his partner directing him, he positioned the Audi with its rear bumper touching that of the other car. They then bundled the injured driver, tracks of blood now smearing his face and neck, back behind the wheel of his car and slammed the door. A moment later, they had the Audi's engine revving before it shot backward, launching the injured man's car toward the cliff.

The Audi shuddered to a halt at the roadside while its occupants watched the other car lurch and buck, crashing over boulders hidden in the heather, its headlight beams soaring skyward before plunging back to earth. The car slowed, seemingly desperate to cling to the safety of the slope, and stopped when its front wheels dropped over the precipice, grounding its underside. It perched there for a moment before the weight of its engine and the crumbling of the cliff edge sent it somersaulting out of sight.

The two killers remained sitting in the Audi when another man appeared from the hillside, jogging past them, lighting his way with a flashlight pointed at the ground. He approached the cliff edge and peered over. On the rocks below, the car lay upside down like a dying turtle, its doors closed, only its wheels above water. The submerged headlights spread an eerie yellow glow around the front of the vehicle for a few moments before they finally faded and died. Satisfied that their job was done, he folded the tarpaulin, taking care that no blood spilled onto the road, and slipped it inside a large, black bin liner. He then stowed it in the boot of the Audi before climbing into the back seat. Not a word was spoken as they sped off into the night.

"This will be some kind o' joke, is it no'?" Sergeant Hamish Macbeth stared Superintendent Daviot straight in the eye. "Have you gone completely doolally?"

"Sergeant Macbeth!" Daviot barked. "You will not use that tone with me! As your senior officer, you will address me with the respect my rank demands!"

"Aye, right," Hamish said, his stare never wavering. "So have you gone completely doolally, *sir*?"

Daviot pursed his lips in anger but had no time to respond before Macbeth charged ahead.

"You can't seriously expect me to police my beat wi' somebody looking like that!" he growled, pointing at the third man in the superintendent's office. The man was wearing a pale blue shirt with a silver star badge above the left breast pocket and sergeant's chevrons on the sleeves. Above the chevrons were neat octagonal shoulder patches with the words "Chicago Police" embracing a representation of the city's seal. "The folk around Lochdubh will never take me seriously ever again."

"Macbeth, I expect you to follow orders!" Daviot fumed. "I expect you to…"

"Maybe I could jump in at this point, sir," said Chicago Police Sergeant James Bland with a calm, pacifying smile. "Hamish, you know I've been to Lochdubh, so I know a little about your people there and I don't want to make any waves."

Hamish looked at Bland. The man had always been

a mystery—part golfing gambler, part stock-market inves-
tor, part globetrotting playboy, and now part cop. What else
was he into? Why was he now standing beside him in front of
Daviot's desk? Why was he back in Scotland?

"How about this?" Bland detached the metal star from his
shirt. "I'm happy to wear something less conspicuous—maybe
one of your Police Scotland black shirts—I'll just pin my star
to it to help explain who I am and why I'm here."

"And just why are you here?" Hamish narrowed his eyes,
delivering the question like a challenge.

"Officially, Sergeant Bland is here as part of an exchange
scheme, learning about the policing methods employed in
Scotland," Daviot explained, holding out a document with a
Police Scotland letterhead. "Our orders are that he is to be
afforded every hospitality and that he is to accompany you as
you go about your normal day-to-day duties."

"And unofficially?" Hamish asked, having scanned the
document.

"Actually, Hamish," Bland said, still smiling, his American
drawl far more relaxed than Daviot's nervous, tense delivery,
"the unofficial part's pretty official, too."

He offered Hamish a document with a UK Government
Home Office heading. Hamish read the text, skipping the
preamble to focus on what he immediately recognized as the
heart of the matter.

"It says here that you're working 'covertly' and I'm to give
you 'every possible assistance in pursuit of the investigation.'"
Hamish glowered at Bland. "What investigation?"

"You recognize this?" Bland took back the Home Office
document, exchanging it for another piece of paper. It was a

printout of a computer spreadsheet showing columns of numbers and, at the bottom of the first column, three names—Vadoit, Serdonna and Ralbi.

"Aye, I mind o' this," Hamish said with a resigned sigh. He now knew exactly why Bland was back in Scotland. "Four people died on account o' this," he added, shaking the spreadsheet. "It damn near got me killed as well!"

"Then you have a vested interest in finding out what it was all about," Bland reasoned.

"I know fine what it was all about!" Hamish could feel another flush of anger spreading from the back of his neck. He could also feel himself being corralled into a situation that was about as far from the simple, peaceful life he enjoyed in Lochdubh as you could get. He felt the problems of the world outside his Highland haven weighing heavy on his shoulders and slumped into a chair, running a hand through his fiery red hair, steadying his temper with a heavy sigh. "It was about secrets, traitors and spies. A coded list o' names and payments—spies paying for secrets from traitors—and the names Daviot, Anderson and Blair as anagrams at the bottom."

"I hope you're not suggesting that myself, DCI Anderson or DCI Blair had anything to do with illicit payments!" spluttered Daviot.

"I don't think that's what Hamish meant at all, sir," said Bland, also taking a seat. "We know the three of you were listed as targets should you have gotten too close to the spy ring. We've no reason to suspect anyone ever paid you a nickel."

"Aye," Hamish agreed. "The traitor Morgan Mackay admitted as much just afore he died."

"I see," Daviot said, stiffly lowering himself into his own

chair, slightly galled that, with neither invitation nor permission, two men of inferior rank had seated themselves in his presence—in his own office, for goodness' sakes!

"But others were paid, Hamish," Bland went on, "and some of them are still out there."

"What does it matter?" Hamish argued. "It's all ancient history now."

"That's not entirely true," Bland said, retrieving the spreadsheet from Hamish. "You see, we cracked the code. We turned the numbers into names—the whole spy ring—we know who they are."

"So why don't you just round them up?"

"It's not that simple. We need help tracking some of them down and we need to do it without anyone knowing we're onto them. You know what these people are capable of when they think they've been cornered."

"That I do." Hamish nodded, thinking of Kate Hibbert, a petty blackmailer who had picked on the wrong victim— Morgan Mackay—and had ended up in a watery grave at the bottom of The Corloch. Then the image of Hannah Thomson ghosted into his mind. The old lady had died of a heart attack—literally frightened to death in her own home by Mackay and a Russian thug. Neither of the women had been involved in the so-called spy ring. "Two women were murdered." Hamish let out a sigh. "I suppose they're what you folk would call 'collateral damage.'"

"Not me, Hamish. I'm not one of them. I'm one of the good guys, remember?"

"Spy or spy catcher, you're all playing the same game and none o' it is any o' my business."

"Protecting the people on your patch—people who have faith in you—is your business, though, isn't it? We believe something's happening within the spy ring. We need to find out exactly what's going on to make sure that no more innocent people get hurt."

"I've enough to do as it is without all o' this cloak-and-dagger malarkey."

"We all have our jobs to do, Sergeant," Daviot said, sounding irritated and impatient. "We all have orders to follow. You, more than any other officer under my command, have to make sure that you follow your orders with as little fuss as possible. Need I remind you how precarious your position is in Lochdubh?"

"Precarious?" Hamish raised an eyebrow. "It's the police station closures you're on about, is it? We had a deal…"

"I agreed to do my utmost to keep you and your home in Lochdubh off the list," Daviot said, pointing a finger at Hamish, "and I will continue to do so, but don't imagine the pressure from above to cut costs ever diminishes."

"Are you threatening me?" Hamish bristled.

"It's not a threat, Macbeth," Daviot said, letting his hand fall to the desk. "We're on the same side. You can rely on me to look after your best interests but if you cause problems, you attract the wrong kind of attention from the powers that be. Life then becomes difficult for both of us. Work with Sergeant Bland to resolve his investigation and we can get back to normal again."

"Sergeant Bland," Hamish said, slowly. "Why you? Why no' a secret service team? Why would a police sergeant be sent all this way to track down a bunch o' spies?"

"I'm a cop all right," Bland replied, "or, at least, it's one of the things I have been. Putting me back in a uniform keeps this all as low-key as possible."

Hamish looked from Daviot to Bland and slowly nodded his head. He knew he had no real choice in the matter but had at least made his feelings clear. Like it or not, he was now lumbered with a partner he didn't want and an assignment that would doubtless drag on through the autumn and beyond. At least this wasn't happening at his busiest time, the height of the Highland tourist season. He got to his feet.

"Aye, well," he said with a resigned shrug, "I suppose we'd better get on wi' it, then."

"We'll need to interview you, sir," said Bland, also standing, "as well as Mr. Anderson and Mr. Blair."

"DCI Anderson and I will put ourselves at your disposal here in Strathbane," said Daviot. "DCI Blair is down in Glasgow. He will be under orders to do the same."

Hamish and Bland then left Daviot at his desk, Bland picking up a large, black holdall from Daviot's outer office. Helen, Daviot's secretary, looked up from her keyboard as they strode past. She expected some insolent quip from Hamish and had been composing a particularly vicious "put-down" ever since she'd booked today's appointment with her boss. He left without a word and, disappointed, she shelved her unused retort in her memory for future use.

Not a word was spoken between Hamish and Bland until they had made their way down into the car park. Hamish pressed a button on his key fob to unlock his Land Rover, then paused, leaning against its side.

"I suppose," he said slowly, "you thought I was being a wee bit unhelpful back there."

"I know you have your reasons," Bland said calmly. "You want a nice, quiet life in Lochdubh and you see me as a threat to that."

"Aye, you're right, but I know you'll do what you have to do whether I'm playing along or not."

"And I know you'll play along because, working alongside me, you can keep an eye on what I'm up to."

"I think we understand each other," Hamish said, with a quiet laugh.

"We do," Bland said, smiling and offering Hamish his hand. "When I was last here we parted as friends. Still friends?"

"Still friends," Hamish confirmed, shaking hands. "And I've no' forgotten that I'm in your debt. When Blair went mad and pointed that gun at me, he might have shot me if you'd no' disarmed him."

"Yeah, I reckon you owe me for that, buddy!" Bland grinned, slinging his bag into the back of the car. "But I'm in no hurry to stand in front of any gunmen, so don't expect me to call in that marker any time soon!"

"Aye, but neither will I forget," Hamish assured him, swinging open the driver's door. "Now let's get the hell out of Strathbane and back home to Lochdubh."

The route from police headquarters to the Lochdubh road took them out of Strathbane's drab city center through an area of shabby low-rise factory buildings made to look all the more dilapidated in the flat light, dulled by the heavy gray clouds lumbering in from the Atlantic.

"Strathbane's not exactly the jewel of the Highlands, is it?" commented Bland, staring out the window at the litter-strewn car park of a disused industrial unit, its few windows boarded up and its gate chained shut.

"It's no' all as bad as this," Hamish replied, shaking his head when he heard his own words. Was he really defending Strathbane? He hated the place. He hated the run-down shopping area, the concrete tower blocks and the seedy backstreets haunted by drug dealers and their prey. Yet it was still part of the Highlands. It was still like a member of the family and families can bicker, quarrel and criticize among themselves, with their own, but when anyone from outside the family has a bad word to say, it's a different story. The family stands together. "There are some nice parts. Superintendent Daviot bides here and he has a nice house. Strathbane suffered when the fishing industry collapsed and nothing new they've tried to get up and running here has ever really worked."

"So, ripe for regeneration, eh? But never a patch on Lochdubh."

"That it's not," Hamish agreed, "and never will be."

The road climbed up out of the town and through a belt of pine trees, emerging onto an area of high moorland where Hamish turned onto the A835 heading toward Inchnadamph.

"This is more the kind of scenery I remember from my last trip to Scotland," Bland said, waving a hand at the steep, rocky hillside on their right and the boggy ground on their left that rose more slowly through countless ponds and lochans to mountain peaks smothered with cloud. The sinister dark blues and grays of the clouds made it look as though scraping the summits had bruised their underbellies. "What's over there, Hamish?"

"That's the Drumrunie Forest wi' the twin peaks o' Cùl

Mòr yonder. It's no' the highest hereabouts, under three thousand feet, but on a good day you can see all the way out to the Isle of Lewis from the top, and Lewis is near forty miles offshore."

"Did you say Drumrunie Forest? I'm not seeing a whole lot of trees out there, bud."

"Aye, well at one time, and we're talking about thousands of years ago, the whole o' Scotland was one massive forest. Here in the northwest there were oak, birch, rowan—all sorts, including the Scots pine, of course."

"Really? The only trees we've come through looked like well-managed forest, like the countryside had been tamed. Up here it's really dramatic—really wild."

"It's wild, right enough, but there are still plenty who live here, crofters and the like. When this was all forest it was properly wild. There were wolves, bears, elk, boar and even big cats like lynx. All o' those are long gone."

"What happened?"

"People. Around six thousand years ago people began burning the forests to create grazing land. Then there was a spot o' what's nowadays called climate change that didn't fare well for some o' the trees. What was left was hacked down over the next three thousand years to build houses and ships, and for fuel."

"All of the original forest is gone?"

"There are massive areas o' new forest but only patches o' the ancient Caledonian Forest still exist. Down south in Fortingall there's a yew tree they say is over five thousand years old."

"Wow. I'd like to go take a look at that."

"Fortingall's down near Aberfeldy," Hamish said, shooting a glance at Bland. "That's near a four-hour drive from here. I thought you were here to catch spies, no' to hit the tourist trail."

"I've never been against combining business with pleasure," Bland said, grinning, "but the old yew tree might have to wait a while longer. I need to fill you in on what we now know about the guys we're looking for."

"Aye, and maybe we can try a bit o' business and pleasure on that front," Hamish responded, peering out through a windscreen now spattered with raindrops at an ever-darkening sky threatening to deliver a deluge. "Once we're back in Lochdubh this evening and I've fed my dog and cat, we can head out to the Italian for a bite to eat. The food there's top notch."

"Sounds good to me," said Bland and the automatic windscreen wipers kicked in, working desperately to clear the mix of giant raindrops and hailstones now battering the car.

By the time they reached Lochdubh, dense curtains of rain were scouring the road and, crossing the stone humpbacked bridge that was the only way into the village, Hamish could see the waters of the River Anstey running fast and black down to the loch. The rocks over which the river usually tumbled, creating lacy white frills, were now completely submerged and the Anstey was threatening to burst its banks.

"River's running pretty high," said Bland, peering down through the gloom.

"Aye," Hamish agreed. "I've no' seen it swell so quickly in a long while."

They drove on into the village, the whitewashed cottages

on the lochside road looming like ghosts in the gloom. When they reached the police station, they made a dash through the rain to the side of the building and the kitchen door. Hamish's dog, Lugs, a large, joyous creature of several colors and numerous breeds, provided his usual, manically enthusiastic welcome, tail waving like a flag, ears flapping like wings as he bounced around their legs. He seemed every bit as happy to welcome Bland, a stranger, as he was to see Hamish. Sonsie, Hamish's cat, was far less generous with her affection. She rubbed herself against Hamish's legs, her purring rumbling like pebbles on a drum. Then she gave Bland a look of pure disdain, turning her back on him with divine indifference and strutting over to sit by her food bowl. She stared at Hamish, blinking twice as though issuing an instruction for him to do his duty.

"I've a bit o' pollack for you, Sonsie, and some venison sausages for you, Lugs," Hamish said, opening the fridge. Lugs barked joyously on hearing the words "venison sausages."

"That's a real big cat," Bland said, leaning against the kitchen sink. "I can understand why there are rumors about her."

"Rumors?" Hamish raised an eyebrow. "Those would be rumors about her being a wildcat, would they?"

"Just what I heard." Bland shrugged.

"It would be illegal to keep a wildcat without a special license and, in any case, no wildcat has ever been tamed." Hamish offered the two undeniable facts to smooth the way for something that was much farther from the truth. "Sonsie's just a big tabby."

"Whatever you say, Hamish." Bland grinned, picking up his bag. "Can I stow this somewhere, then maybe we can grab that bite to eat at your Italian place."

"Upstairs on the left. We'll drive to the restaurant. Willie will have a table for us." He glanced out the window. "Any table we like, I should think. Nobody else will be out on a night like this."

Half an hour later they burst in through the door of the Napoli restaurant, shaking rainwater from their fluorescent, hi-vis Police Scotland rain jackets, although both had changed into casual clothes rather than their uniforms. Willie Lamont looked up from where he was polishing one of the establishment's complement of empty tables.

"Hamish, come away in. Good to see you!" Willie called cheerfully.

"Willie, this is Sergeant James Bland from Chicago," Hamish said, hanging his jacket on a coat stand near the door. "He's going to be working wi' me for a bit."

"*Benvenuto*," Willie said, shaking Bland's hand.

"*È un piacere conoscervi*," Bland replied smoothly in Italian. Momentarily paralyzed by a mix of panic and confusion, Willie gave him the fixed, frozen smile of a cartoon character who's just been whacked with a frying pan but isn't yet feeling the effect.

"Okay if we sit here?" Hamish said, parking himself at a table by the window.

"I'll bring you the menu," Willie said, recovering sufficiently to scurry off to the bar area.

"Willie's no' very good at talking Italian," Hamish said in a low voice. "In fact, he gets his English words mixed up as well, but he tries hard."

"I can help him practice a bit," Bland said with a smile. "I've spent some time in Italy."

Willie returned and offered Hamish a menu, recommending the starter of "proscoosho di Parma."

"I think that's *prosciutto di Parma*," Bland pointed out.

"Aye, that'll be it," Willie agreed, handing Bland a menu.

"We'll have a bottle o' your Valpolicella, Willie," Hamish said, looking to Bland who gave an approving nod.

"Excellent choice!" Willie congratulated Hamish on choosing exactly the same wine that he always chose, while scribbling unnecessarily on a pad. "Una bottic“kleyo."

"A bottle is *una bottiglia*," said Bland, and Willie nodded an acknowledgment, although looking slightly peeved at having been corrected again.

"And I'll have the spaghetti wi' meatballs," Hamish announced, once again ordering his usual. Bland opted for that as well, holding out his menu for Willie to take.

"*Grazie*," said Bland.

"Pricko," Willie responded.

"I think you mean *prego*," said Bland.

"Of course," Willie said, smiling politely then hurrying to the kitchen muttering softly to himself, "I ken fine what I meant…Pricko."

"Willie used to be my constable," Hamish said. "Then he married Lucia, whose parents own this place, and came to work here."

"She must be quite a woman for him to give up his career."

"She is that," Hamish said, nodding, "but, truth be told, Willie's heart was never in being a police officer. He's far happier here."

"I seem to recall that another two of your guys work at the big hotel that I stayed in on the edge of the village."

"Aye, Freddy's the chef at the Tommel Castle and Silas works security. Both o' them were my constables at one time. I've another one, Dick Fraser, now runs a bakery business in Braikie wi' his wife, Anka."

"Yeah, I met Dick on my last visit, too. It's good to know that you have people in the area that you can trust. We might need them."

"No!" Hamish waved a hand across the table as though pushing that thought straight through the window, out into the storm. "I've seen what these people you're after are like, and there's no way I'm putting any of my friends in any kind o' danger."

"I'm with you there, buddy. We don't want that. All I meant was that it will be useful to have eyes and ears around the area while we're tracking down the bad guys. You know people around here. They trust you. That's why I need you to help me find the men on our list."

"So who are they?"

Bland fell silent when Willie appeared with the wine and made a show of opening the bottle and offering a taste before pouring two glasses.

"*Grazie*, Willie," said Bland, smiling.

Willie looked at him for an instant, finally deciding that Bland was trying to be friendly rather than patronizing, and gave a slight nod.

"*Prego*," he said, taking care to pronounce the word just as Bland had done, before returning to the kitchen.

"We've identified a dozen names on the spreadsheet," Bland explained. "Over the years, four have died of natural causes—some of these people are getting on a bit, you know? Of the remaining eight, two have died very recently—quite soon after you got your hands on the spreadsheet—in circumstances that can only be described as highly suspicious. I think it's a bit of a coincidence to have two such deaths just when it looked like the spy ring was about to be exposed."

"The only really believable thing I ever heard any TV detective say was that, when it comes to murder, there's no such thing as coincidence."

"Too true," Bland said, laughing. "Proving they were murdered isn't really what I'm here for, but taking a look at the deaths, talking to known associates, might help us to track down the rest of the outfit."

"Who were the dead pair?"

"The guy down in Glasgow was Edward Chalmers. He used to work at the Royal Navy's submarine base at Faslane. He apparently committed suicide at his home in Glasgow by setting fire to himself."

"That's a hellish way to die," Hamish said with a grimace. "No' the way most folk would choose to end their lives, but a braw way to destroy any evidence of foul play."

"Exactly. The second dead guy was Callum Graham, who seems to have driven his car off a cliff somewhere south of here, near Lochcarron."

"Aye, I heard about that," Hamish said, rubbing his chin. "It was at Applecross only a few days ago, was it no'? I've a pal, Lachlan, works at the police station in Lochcarron. We can ask him about yon car crash."

"That could be a good place to start."

Willie arrived bearing two huge plates piled high with steaming pasta, glistening in a rich tomato sauce, tempting meatballs peeking out from behind a veil of spaghetti strands. He made a great show of offering them grated *"Parmigiano"* from a small bowl and *"pepe nero"* from a large, phallic-looking pepper grinder, then retreated to the kitchen again, pleased that Bland appeared to approve of his pronunciation.

"So what about the final six?" Hamish asked, once they were alone. "Surely they're no' that hard to find if you have their names."

"I think I've traced one of them," Bland said, tucking into his meal. "Hey, this is real good…but we need to approach him in a way that won't alert the others. Trouble is, I don't really know who the others are. I have names but that's about it. One of them has gone to ground—dropped off the radar completely. The others—well, the names we have could be phony because there's no trace of them at all."

"I can probably come up wi' some way o' getting to talk to the one you've traced," Hamish said, twirling pasta on his fork. "I'll see if I recognize any o' the others. You can show me the list when we're back at the station."

"Your station's also your home," Bland said, and Hamish nodded, his cheek bulging with a mouthful of meatball. "What was all that between you and Daviot about stations being shut down?"

"There's ay a list sitting on somebody's desk," Hamish said, having swallowed hard to clear his mouth. "There's ay somebody wi' one o' the top police jobs, trying to balance his books. There's ay a plan to save money by shutting down what some see as wasteful rural stations. No' so long ago there were police stations all around the north coast. Folk could go there when they had a problem and somebody was ay there for them—they could rely on their local police. Now a police station's a rare sight, heading for extinction like the lynx and the elk, and those that are left aren't all permanently manned. Ower at Dornoch, the police station used to have an inspector, a sergeant and a dozen constables. Now it's gone."

"So you do whatever you have to, to keep Lochdubh open, to keep policing at the heart of your community."

"I suppose so," Hamish agreed, "but more than anything, it's my home."

They ate in silence for a few minutes before Hamish reached for the bottle to top them up with a second glass of wine, and his phone rang.

"Hamish! We're on the bridge!" a voice cried through the thrash of torrential rain and the heavy boom of fast-moving water. "It's broke! The bridge is broke!"

"Mrs. Patel?" Hamish said, getting to his feet. "You mean the bridge over the Anstey?"

"Aye, the van's stuck and the bridge is going...!"

"We'll be right there!" Hamish called, reaching for his jacket and heading for the door.

"I'll keep this warm for you!" Willie shouted, appearing as if by magic to spirit their plates away just as his only two customers ran out into the rain.

Hamish raced along the lochside road in the Land Rover, blue lights flashing and siren wailing.

"Had trouble with the bridge before?" Bland asked.

"No' as far as I can remember, but there's no' been any kind o' maintenance on that auld bridge for years, so maybe this was just a matter o' time."

They slammed to a halt just short of the river where Mrs. Patel stood at the side of the road, waving and pointing to the bridge. Somewhere behind the dazzling glare of its headlights, Hamish could make out the shape of a van slouched sideways at an unnatural angle. He jumped out and strode over to Mrs. Patel.

"Mrs. Patel—is Mr. Patel in the van?" he said, raising his voice above the howl of the storm.

"Aye! Please get him out o' there, Hamish!" she wailed. "The van's stuck but he won't leave it. We've been to the cash-and-carry in Strathbane and we've near a fortnight's worth o' stock in it!"

"Get in the Land Rover, Mrs. Patel," Hamish said. "We'll get him off the bridge."

With Bland at his side, he ran the few short yards to the bridge, hauling a flashlight from the pocket of his rain jacket. He could hear the frantic revving of the van's engine accompanied by the useless spinning of its rear wheels.

"Take it easy, Mr. Patel!" Hamish yelled through the driver's window. "Let us have a wee look!"

Bland was already at the rear of the van with his own flashlight and grabbed Hamish's arm as he approached to stop him going any further.

"Half the middle section of the bridge has vanished!" he shouted above the noise of the rain and the rushing water. He played his torch beam across a dark gap, below which they could see a massive tree trunk wedged under the bridge. "That thing must have hit the bridge like a battering ram!"

The van's rear wheels were floundering in the gap, spinning in the air. A couple of stones from the side wall detached themselves and disappeared into the water.

"The whole bridge is starting to crumble under its own weight!" Hamish shouted, turning toward the van again. He yanked open the door and dragged a protesting Mr. Patel out into the rain. "It's no' safe here!" he warned and, each taking an arm, he and Bland half-ran, half-carried Mr. Patel down to the Land Rover, bundling him into the back seat, where his wife threw her arms around him.

"We can use the Land Rover's winch to haul the van clear o' the bridge," Hamish said, grabbing a remote-control handset from the glove box. "James, stay here wi' the car just in case."

Moving to the front of the car, he released the winch hook, using the handset to start the motor reeling out the cable. Carrying the cable back through the rain toward the bridge, he hooked it securely to a towing point beneath the van's front bumper. He then pressed a button on the handset to reverse the winch motor and it began slowly dragging the van forward, heaving its rear wheels out of the gap. With the wheels back on a solid surface, the van began slithering toward the bridge's side wall. Hamish jumped into the cab. He tried starting the engine, but it wouldn't fire. Then, coming from behind him, he heard the ominous rumble of falling masonry.

"Hamish!" Bland roared. "Get out of there! The whole bridge is going!"

CHAPTER TWO

Don't you think that any secret course is an unworthy one?
> Charles Dickens, *David Copperfield*

The van lurched when the bridge behind it fell away, leaving the rear wheels unsupported once again. Hamish hauled on the steering wheel to try to guide the front end away from the bridge wall but lost all control when there came a resounding crash and he was flung back in the seat, the whole van tipping backward, starting to slide into the roaring river. He felt a surge of panic. If the van toppled into the Anstey, he'd be stuck inside! The drop into the water wasn't far but he'd be battered from one end of the cab to the other, and if he survived that, then he'd be in the freezing water with the van rolling over and over. He'd never be able to get out! His mind ran through a high-speed nightmare of horrifying images. He saw himself trapped in a tangle of buckled metal. There was water everywhere. He was struggling to keep his face above the surface. He could barely breathe. No—that wasn't going to happen! It was time to abandon ship!

He reached for the door handle, but the door wouldn't budge. It was already hard against the bridge wall. The only way out was through the passenger door. He heaved his lanky frame to the other side of the cab. His rain-jacket pocket caught on the gear lever, holding him back. He reached desperately for the door, only to be hurled against the dashboard when the van suddenly pitched forward. There was a horrendous crunch and screech, the bodywork grinding against the side wall until the vehicle slithered down off the bridge toward the safety of the road. Hamish looked up to see Bland behind the wheel of his Land Rover, reversing away from the bridge, hauling the van to the sanctuary of solid ground.

He struggled back into the driver's seat and leant on the steering wheel, breathing hard, trying to banish from his mind all thoughts of the watery demise he had so narrowly escaped. Bland stopped the Land Rover but Hamish could feel the winch still dragging the van toward it. He reached down to where the remote control had fallen to the floor and switched off the winch.

"That was a close shave!" Bland said, wrenching open the buckled and dented van door. "Hope I didn't burn out your winch hauling you out like that."

"It...it'll be fine," Hamish replied, pulling his thoughts together. "They build these things tough. We'll have to turn the Land Rover round and tow the van to the village."

"No problem," Bland said, wiping rain from his face. "I'll unhitch the winch."

"Aye," Hamish said, then raised his voice above the

pounding of the rain to reach Bland, who was already at the winch hook. "James, I...I mean...just, thanks."

"No worries," Bland called back, grinning. "Teamwork got the job done!"

They walked back through the rain to the Land Rover, Hamish carrying the cable, the winch faithfully reeling it in. Once they had towed the van to the Patels' post-office-*cum*-mini-supermarket and Hamish had assured Mr. Patel that he would provide a full account of everything that had happened for the Patels' insurers, Hamish and Bland sat for a moment in the police car.

"I guess you've got a lot of paperwork to do now," Bland said.

"There's ay the paperwork," Hamish said quietly, staring out into the rain as though contemplating his brush with death back on the bridge.

"You feel okay?" Bland asked.

"No," Hamish replied slowly, then started the engine. "I feel hungry—and Willie will have our pasta ready waiting for us."

An hour later, they were back in the police station, having eaten their fill but having drunk very little of the wine, which Willie had given them to take away. Hamish put the bottle by the kitchen sink and fussed over Lugs and Sonsie before opening his laptop computer to file a quick report about the bridge collapse. Then both men settled into chairs at the kitchen table.

"So," said Bland, opening a beige folder he had fetched from his room, "these are the men I was telling you about in the restaurant. I like to think of them as 'The Despicable Dozen.'"

He showed Hamish a sheet of paper with a list of twelve names.

Frederick Williams	deceased (natural causes)
Geoffrey Linton	deceased (natural causes)
Stephen Kennedy	deceased (natural causes)
Colin Murphy	deceased (natural causes)
Edward Chalmers	deceased (house fire)
Callum Graham	deceased (car crash)
Alex Caldwell	whereabouts unknown
Dennis McGill	last known address Thurso
Kenneth Robb	last known address Durness
William McAllister	whereabouts unknown
James Smith	whereabouts unknown
John Martin	whereabouts unknown

"None o' these names ring any bells," Hamish said, scanning the list. "How about we try a wee dram to see if that helps? I've a drop o' the good stuff in the cupboard."

He retrieved a bottle of Glenmorangie single malt along with two glasses from a kitchen cabinet and poured them each a generous measure. They clinked glasses, took a sip, and Bland began passing a selection of mugshots across the table.

"This is Williams. Until he retired, he was a civilian maintenance engineer at the Royal Navy's submarine base at Faslane."

"Don't recognize him," Hamish said, studying the photograph, "but Faslane is on the Gare Loch. That's two hundred miles south—way off my patch."

"I reckoned you wouldn't know these guys," Bland said, placing another photo on the table, "but we may as well take a look. This is Linton, also a civilian at Faslane. He worked in the personnel department—human resources."

Hamish shook his head and savored his whisky.

"Kennedy and Murphy both worked at the Holy Loch when the U.S. Navy had submarines based there…"

"Don't know either of them," Hamish said.

"Chalmers was an electrician. He was a civilian worker at Faslane, too. Graham was a teacher. He lived near Lochcarron."

Hamish stared at the black-and-white photographs, searching for a flicker of recognition, but saw only strangers.

"We have no photo of Caldwell and know nothing about him. McGill is a retired engineer. He worked at Dounreay and lives in Thurso. Robb is a laborer and farmhand. He's in Durness."

Hamish picked up the photo of Robb, staring intently at it, but dropped it back on the table with a frustrated shake of his head.

"McAllister, Smith and Martin may all be fake names. We got nothing on them."

Bland scattered a few more photographs on the table. They showed protestors demonstrating near the gates to a military base, closely observed by a number of police officers.

"These shots show demonstrators at the Faslane CND Peace Camp. Various members of the Dozen have shown up there over the years. There have been campaigners on that site since 1982."

"Aye, one o' Scotland's proudest records." Hamish smiled. "The longest-running peace-camp protest ever. You have to admire their commitment and...wait a minute...I know that face."

"That photo's from 1989," Bland said, staring at the back of the picture while Hamish held it up to examine the image of a young woman at the front of a crowd. She was brandishing a homemade placard that read "NO TO NUKES!"

"Can't quite place her," Hamish said, his brow furrowed with concentration. Then his attention was caught by another photograph. "I'd ken that scunner anywhere, though!" He snatched the picture from the table, jabbing a finger at the figure of a police officer standing watching a protest, his hands thrust deep in his pockets. "That's Blair! Younger, no' quite so fat and still in uniform—a sergeant."

"If he was there," Bland said, gathering the photographs, "maybe he'll be able to give us something more on the people in the photos."

"Blair wouldn't give you the crud off his boots unless there was something in it for him."

"Well, when we interview him, we can make sure there's something in it for him—or at least we can make sure he *thinks* there's something in it for him!" Bland grinned.

"So, we've got Blair, Daviot and Jimmy Anderson to talk to, then McGill in Thurso and Robb in Durness."

"I reckon we'll be able to pick some tips from them on how to track down the four we don't have addresses for."

"Maybe, and we also need to talk to Lachlan down at Lochcarron. He should be able to point us in the direction of Callum Graham's family or known associates. Might be a lead or two there."

"That could be real useful. Of course, first we have to get out of Lochdubh."

"Aye, the bridge being down will cause a right stramash in the village. We'll have to deal wi' that in the morn, no doubt. Right now, I'm about ready for bed."

The Jacobite was a dark, musty bar hidden in the bowels of an old drovers' inn. Three centuries ago, Highlanders walking their cattle to the lowland markets in the central belt had drunk, quarreled and fought beneath its low ceilings, and it was said to be haunted by an assassin loyal to Bonnie Prince Charlie. He had been paid to eliminate the enemies of noblemen who supported the Jacobite cause and he had used the bar as a secret lair from where he plied his deadly trade. A barmaid who fell in love with the mysterious stranger ultimately betrayed him out of jealousy when he seduced her younger sister. He died with a dirk in his heart, two kinsmen of his aristocratic victims ambushing him at the entrance to the bar. Locals said he'd since been seen many times, sitting quietly in the darkest corner, biding his time, watching for the barmaid, patiently waiting to exact his revenge on the woman who had denounced him.

The Jacobite, therefore, was an appropriately sinister meeting place for the two men sitting at a dimly lit table, huddled over pints of ale as dark as their intent.

"So where is the auld bugger hiding?" asked the first.

"As far as I can tell, it's an auld croft in the middle o' nowhere near Drumbeg," his companion replied.

"That's no' much to go on, is it? Unapool's near Drumbeg.

Lochinver's near Drumbeg. Even Strathbane's no' that far away."

"We need to get more out o' the woman. She must know where it is."

"Aye, he'll come crawling out o' his hidey-hole if he thinks she's in danger. We need to make her think we'll kill her if we can't get to him. Then she'll find a way to contact him."

"And if she doesn't?"

"Then we have to get rid o' her anyway."

The other man took a swig of beer, wiped his mouth on the back of his hand and let out a short sigh.

"We can't go on like this," he said in a voice that was little more than a whisper. "We won't get away wi' it forever. How many more have to die?"

"As many as it takes! It's us or them! You know what the foreigners are like. We do as they tell us or we're dead meat. Finish your pint. We need to pay a visit to the woman."

"Macbeth! Where the devil are you, you lazy scoundrel?"

There was no mistaking either the voice of Colonel George Halburton-Smythe or the terse irritation in his delivery. Hamish had been enjoying his breakfast of sausage, bacon and eggs, especially given that Bland had prepared it, but paused with a chunk of sausage on his fork. He looked expectantly toward the open kitchen door. Lugs, sitting to attention by Hamish's chair, cocked an ear toward the approaching footsteps, although his eyes never left the hovering sausage.

"I should have known I'd find you here!" The colonel appeared in the doorway, his face flushed almost as much from the vigorous walk from the Tommel Castle Hotel as it was from his foul temper.

"Aye, that you should," Hamish replied, casually popping the sausage into his mouth and continuing to talk with his mouth full, "this being a police station and me being a police officer, after all."

Lugs tilted his head in disappointment but remained at attention, ever hopeful that there might be more on Hamish's plate. The colonel continued his tirade.

"Don't be impertinent, Sergeant!" he barked. He was a small man, but there was no mistaking his military bearing. He wore a checked shirt with a regimental tie, a tweed jacket and flannels with creases so sharp they could probably have cut Hamish's next chunk of sausage. "I mean in here having breakfast when there is urgent work waiting for you out there!"

"I guess you must mean the bridge, sir," said Bland, and the colonel noticed him for the first time. There was a flicker of confusion in his eyes before the American accent and the familiar face finally pried open the door to the colonel's memory vault.

"Mr. Bland," he said, smiling politely and offering his hand. "I must admit you caught me rather off guard. I certainly wasn't expecting to see you here."

"No, last time I was in these parts my accommodation was far more luxurious," said Bland, standing to shake hands. "Your hotel was one of the highlights of my trip."

"Well, thank you," the colonel said, switching from flaming fury to oily charm in the blink of an eye. "We would love to have you stay with us again. Why are you here and dressed like...?"

"A cop?" Bland laughed, patting his hand on the Chicago Police star attached to his black Police Scotland shirt. "My apologies for catching you unawares, sir, but I'm here precisely because I *am* a cop. I had such a wonderful time here on vacation that I managed to wangle a spot on an exchange course so that I could come back again."

"I see," the colonel said, his eyes flitting from Hamish, who was mopping egg yolk off his plate with a piece of bread, to Lugs, who was convinced the eggy bread would be coming his way, and back to Bland. "Yes, yes, we had those sorts of exchanges in the army. Jolly good for learning how another chap gets the job done."

"Would you care for a cup of coffee, Colonel?" Hamish asked, standing to reach for the coffee pot. "I'll be having one myself while Sergeant Bland finishes his breakfast."

"Thank you, most kind." The colonel accepted a mug of coffee and sat when Hamish indicated a vacant chair at the table. He took his time to evaluate the situation. He'd been unexpectedly outflanked but he needed to rally his thoughts, regroup, take the initiative and go back on the offensive. "But see here, Macbeth, you really need to get cracking and do something about the bridge."

"I'm a police officer, no' an engineer," Hamish said, taking a swig of coffee. "Rebuilding the bridge is a job for the regional council, no' the police."

"Don't try shirking your responsibilities like that!" replied the colonel. "I have guests at my hotel who will be leaving tomorrow morning and others who will be arriving tomorrow afternoon. How are they supposed to do that when there's no way in or out of Lochdubh?"

"Well, we could ask Archie Maclean to use his fishing boat to ferry people over to the landing stage near the foot o' Hurdy's Glen."

"But what about their cars? Maclean's smelly old fishing boat isn't big enough to take any vehicles! And what are they supposed to do when they disembark at the landing stage? How do they get home from there?"

"Aye, that's a bit of a pickle, right enough..."

"You need to talk to the council to get this sorted out!" The colonel banged his coffee mug down on the table.

"I'm working on it," Hamish said, calmly. "I've already been in touch wi' the council this morning."

"Nonsense!" snapped the colonel. "It's barely eight o'clock and none of those work-shy layabouts at the council offices are at their desks before ten!"

Hamish's phone rang and he fished it out of his pocket before having a brief conversation that ended with, "You're on your way? Aye, the weather's holding fair here, sir. That's grand. I'll see you at nine o'clock."

He rang off, looking across the table at the colonel.

"That could solve all our problems," Hamish announced. "The man I just spoke to says he can build us a new bridge."

"A new bridge?" the colonel replied, frowning. "When does he plan on starting the work?"

"He says he can start later today and have it done by this afternoon."

"Utter claptrap!" the colonel replied with a snort. "Any idiot knows it will take weeks to rebuild the bridge!" He narrowed his eyes and gave Hamish a suspicious, sideways look. "Are you trying to make a fool of me in front of Mr. Bland? It doesn't do to play games with me, Macbeth. Need I remind you that I am a personal friend of Superintendent Daviot?"

"You need not. That's not something I'm ever likely to forget," Hamish replied. "So, if I can sort out a bridge for your guests, would it be worth a table for dinner in your hotel restaurant?"

"Of course, if they can drive in and out of Lochdubh, but you'll never manage that, Macbeth," the colonel said, shaking his head. "Just let me know what emergency measures you *can* put in place. I want a progress report by the end of play today. Now I must get back. I have guests who need to be reassured that we are making every effort to ensure that they are *not* trapped here in Lochdubh!"

The colonel marched out the door to be confronted by Sonsie, who treated him to a sinister combination of hiss and growl before allowing him to shuffle carefully around her.

"I can't help thinking that you're skating on thin ice by winding the colonel up like that." Bland chuckled, helping Hamish to wash up their breakfast dishes.

"Now, what is it would make you think I was winding him up?" Hamish asked, smiling.

Bland laughed, shaking his head, unwilling to take whatever bait Hamish might be offering.

"Well, we'll see how the bridge thing works out," Hamish said. "In the meantime, we'd better take a wee dander along there and have a look at the damage in the daylight."

＊ ＊ ＊

Ten minutes later they were strolling along the waterfront toward the bridge. The rain had stopped earlier that morning, leaving high clouds to drift in from the Atlantic, heading east and breaking apart under the kind of persistent autumn sun that still offered enough warmth to persuade you to leave your jacket at home. A light breeze wafted in off the loch, bringing a briny tang to air which, when the gentle gusts faded, mingled with the sweet smell of rain-soaked vegetation, the scent of heather from the hillsides and the faint perfume of late-flowering roses in cottage front gardens.

Hamish breathed in great lungfuls of the fresh air feeling, not for the first time, that there was no finer place to live than Lochdubh. He was wearing his white police shirt and his service belt but hadn't bothered with the protective utility vest. Bland was in his black, zip-necked shirt, the modern style of uniform that Hamish had always resisted adopting. He maintained that the black Police Scotland shirt, shapeless black cargo trousers and black tactical boots made him look more like a special forces binman than a police officer. He stuck to the old uniform, especially when he was on home turf. He also wore his traditional peaked cap, as opposed to the cheap-looking baseball cap that had been issued to Bland. When Superintendent Daviot accused him of being resistant to change, Hamish pointed out that he used a computer and an iPad, and carried the latest kind of smartphone, but he didn't want to be seen as part of a police force to which the people on his patch found it difficult to relate. They liked the way he presented himself in a traditional uniform, but saw the electronic gadgets as tools to support his general laziness.

In his position, caught between the demands of his superiors and the expectations of those who lived around Lochdubh, he had long since concluded that it was impossible to please everyone, so he mainly focused on pleasing himself.

"It really is beautiful around here, Hamish," said Bland, looking out over the loch to where cloud shadows were creeping across the mountainside on the far shore.

"Aye, it's a braw place to live, but being a police officer here means you're never off duty. Everyone knows exactly who you are, even when you're no' in uniform, and everyone feels free to bring you their troubles at any time o' the day."

"That must be pretty exhausting."

"It's no' so bad really. I wouldn't want it any other way. Folk around here are no' like any others." Hamish paused, spotting two small, yet unmistakable figures in the distance. "Apart from those two. They're exactly like each other."

Approaching at pace, marching immaculately in unison, were Nessie and Jessie Currie, each twin wearing a beige raincoat buttoned up to the neck, pink-framed glasses and a transparent plastic rain bonnet covering identically permed gray hair.

"One day," Hamish said quietly to Bland, "I'll work out how to walk along the waterfront here without bumping into this pair."

Bland chuckled, then braced himself as Nessie's strident voice hit them like the opening blast from an over-enthusiastic bagpiper.

"Hamish Macbeth!" she skirled. "What are you doing here ambling around when we're all in fear for our lives!"

"Fear for our lives!" crowed Jessie, who had the intensely

annoying habit of repeating the last thing her sister said, like the pervasive, empty-room echo of a tightly wound cuckoo clock.

"Good morning, ladies," Hamish said, with a pleasant smile, "and what would it be that was putting us all in such terrible danger today? We've no' acquired a monster in Loch Dubh like the one in Loch Ness have we?"

"If the one in Loch Ness is called Nessie, we'd have to call the one here Doobie!" Bland laughed. "Sounds kinda cool."

Nessie glowered at him, wondering whether he realized that she shared her name with the camera-shy creature in Loch Ness and if he was poking fun at her. She decided that he didn't, and he wasn't.

"And who might you be?" she demanded. "I think we've seen you before!"

"Seen you before!"

"You may well have done, ma'am," Bland replied, instantly converting his laughter into an amiable smile. "I'm James Bland. I spent some time here a while back on vacation. I loved your town so much I jumped at the chance to come back and work with Sergeant Macbeth."

"But you're not a Scottish policeman," Nessie pointed out, squinting at Bland's badge. "Chicago Police it says there. An American. I thought as much. You'll have no police powers here. Chicago is three and a half thousand miles in that direction."

"That direction." Jessie nodded in agreement, both sisters pointing toward the distant mouth of the loch.

"I'd say you've got a pretty impressive grasp of geography," Bland congratulated them. "I'll be heading back before too long but in the meantime I'm here to help Sergeant Macbeth as best I can."

"Well, he's going to need all the help he can get," Nessie said with an emphatic nod that was immediately mirrored by her sister. "He's got to deal with the Anstey Bridge Disaster!"

"Anstey Bridge Disaster!"

"Och, it's a disaster now, is it?" Hamish said slowly. "There was me thinking it was just a wee bridge collapse."

"That's the trouble with you, Hamish Macbeth—you never think of anything much beyond your next meal!" Nessie berated Hamish. "In the meantime, the food will run out and we'll starve to death!"

"Starve to death!" Jessie's voice rose in a hysterical shriek that ended in a high-pitched hiccup. Her sister scowled at her.

"None o' us are likely to starve to death while there are sheep on the hillside, fish in the loch, chickens in our sheds and, to the best of my knowledge, enough chocolate biscuits in Mr. Patel's store to keep you supplied for months wi' your afternoon tea," Hamish said.

"Chocolate biscuits? Who can afford those at Patel's prices?" Nessie sounded appalled. "We bake our own shortbread!"

"Our own shortbread!" echoed Jessie, attempting to compensate for her shrieking with a voice that sounded like a badly tuned double bass.

"But that doesn't change the fact that we can't use the bridge!" Nessie continued, ignoring her sister. "We are all stranded in Lochdubh!"

"Stranded in Lochdubh!" Jessie repeated with a sob, as though she were about to burst into tears. Her sister tutted at her.

"Aye, I can see how that might be a problem," Hamish

agreed, thoughtfully stroking his chin, "if you ever actually went anywhere, but you two never really leave the village."

"That's beside the point!" Nessie snapped. "Lochdubh needs its bridge!"

"Needs its bridge!"

"I understand the urgency right enough," Hamish assured them. "By the end of this afternoon a new bridge will be erected."

"This afternoon? I don't believe a word of it, Hamish Macbeth." Nessie gave a tight shake of her head. "Who could handle such an erection?"

"Handle such a..." Jessie stopped and glared at her sister with wide eyes and raised eyebrows. Realization dawned on her face and Nessie looked appalled at the double meaning in what she had just said. She tugged at the sleeves of her raincoat, then held her head high.

"You're talking a load of rubbish!" she said indignantly. "An absolute load of blethers and havers!"

"Blethers and havers!" echoed Jessie, clearly relieved to be dealing with more acceptable vocabulary. The twins then took their leave, marching past the two police officers.

"Salt o' the earth, those two," Hamish said, watching them go. "They never miss a thing that goes on around here. I could rely on them for anything."

"Really?" said Bland. "Then why were you giving them all that crap about a new bridge by this afternoon?"

"Because I'm fairly confident it will happen," Hamish replied, seeing the skeptical expression on Bland's face. "You don't believe me? Well, you're a gambling man, James. Care for a wee wager?"

"Not a chance," Bland said, eyeing Hamish suspiciously. "I've played a fair bit of poker in my time and I'm pretty good at reading my opponents. Somehow I get the impression that you've got more than one ace up your sleeve."

"Suit yourself." Hamish shrugged, glancing at his watch. "Let's get a move on, though. We need to get round to the bridge."

When they arrived at the riverbank, the Anstey was flowing just as high and as fast as it had been the night before. The two ends of the arched stone bridge were still standing, although much of the central section was missing, creating a gap like missing teeth in the smile of an old friend. The tree trunk that had caused most of the damage was now stranded on some shingle at the mouth of the river by the loch. On the far side of the bridge stood a large man with a bushy beard. He was wearing a brown anorak and leaning against a muddy pickup truck. He waved to Hamish, who grinned and waved back, holding up his phone.

"That's my cousin Finlay," Hamish explained. "He's the local council's engineering officer. I spoke to him earlier."

He pressed a redial number on his phone and Finlay raised his own phone to his ear. Bland could hear Finlay's voice booming out above the noise of the river, making the phones almost redundant.

"It's no' as bad as it looks, Hamish," Finlay said, pointing to the bridge. "The center section has come out fairly clean. I can't see any cracks or evidence o' serious structural damage on what's left."

"You had the bridge listed as an important local landmark,"

Hamish reminded his cousin. "Will it be rebuilt just as it was?"

"That's the idea," Finlay confirmed. "I can divert a team from a job up near Braikie and get them here this afternoon. We should be able to reuse some of the original stones, so they can start fishing them out o' the water. Organizing scaffolding, masons and a full construction squad will take a wee bit longer. The whole job's going to take a while—we're talking weeks, not days, Hamish."

"Aye, and that's where these lads come in," Hamish said pointing to a black saloon car that had pulled up alongside Finlay's pickup. The driver, a young soldier, waved to Hamish as he got out, then stood to attention and saluted as two officers disembarked from the rear seats.

"That young laddie is Keith Bain," Hamish explained to Bland. "I met him a while back, when you were last here, on a murder investigation. The officer on the left is his CO, Captain Munro, wi' the Black Watch at Ardersier. The other officer is Captain Munro's brother, a major wi' the Royal Engineers based no' far from Ardersier at Kinloss."

Finlay handed his phone to Captain Munro.

"Good morning, Sergeant Macbeth," said the captain. "Looks like the storm made a bit of a mess of your bridge."

"Aye, it did that, sir," Hamish replied. "Finlay will fix the bridge, but I was hoping the major might be able to help us out in the meantime."

"Let's see, shall we?" The captain handed the phone to his brother.

"Thank you for coming all this way, sir," Hamish said. "Will you be able to do anything for us?"

"I think so, Sergeant," the major said. "Actually, you're in luck, because we have a whole consignment of kit ready to move out of Kinloss. I'll sort out the paperwork. Permission from the top brass won't be a problem—public relations, working with the community and all that. We'll get our boys up here later today."

"I was hoping you'd say that, sir," said Hamish. "I saw your lads put on a bridge-laying demonstration in competition wi' some other engineers at the Strathbane Highland Games no' so long ago. They spanned a gap wider than this in no time at all and won hands down."

"They did indeed, Sergeant," the major said, proudly, "and they set a new record. Just under eight and a half minutes for the whole job, as I recall."

"Will you be able to do that here, sir?"

"Once the trucks arrive and our equipment is set up, it shouldn't take too long," the major confirmed. "We can go from this fairly flat area at the bend in the road here, across to the little car park by the picnic area on your side. We'll have to take down the car park wall, of course."

"That's grand, sir," Hamish said. "I can get a crew working on that over here. If you can liaise wi' Finlay on that side, then we can start to get things moving."

Hamish talked with his cousin and the officers, establishing how best to close off the old bridge and direct traffic onto the new one while Bland looked on in wonder, thankful that he had followed his instincts in declining Hamish's suggestion of a wager.

Three hours later, Hamish had a team of locals carefully dismantling the car park wall one stone at a time, photographing the operation as they went and labeling each stone so that it could eventually be put back just as it was. Mrs. Wellington, the minister's wife, and Angela Brodie, wife of the local doctor, set up an urn to provide tea and coffee while Mrs. Patel brought bread and sundry items from the store to make sandwiches. Hamish and Bland used crush barriers and traffic cones to redirect any eventual traffic away from the old bridge toward where the new temporary one would be and then accepted mugs of coffee while watching a convoy of army trucks arrive on the opposite side of the river.

The trucks were hauling trailers laden with green-painted steel beams and girders, the constituent elements of a bridge that the major assured them would easily "take the weight of a main battle tank or whatever else you care to throw at it." Teams of soldiers were busy unloading the trucks as Hamish and Bland looked out across the water, enjoying their coffee. It was then that the Currie twins arrived, each carrying an identical cake tin.

"Homemade shortbread," said Nessie, placing her tin on the table. "Freshly baked."

"Freshly baked," said Jessie, placing her tin beside her sister's.

They each politely thanked Mrs. Wellington for the cup of tea she offered before joining the increasing throng of locals on seats and benches in the picnic area, watching the bridge take shape. It seemed as though everyone had turned out to see the birth of their new bridge. Soldiers who had been lifted across the river in the bucket of a giant crane prepared the site in the car park and then the bridge began to grow, assembled section by section on the far side of the river and gradually pushed out across the water. Finally, the steel of the bridge touched the tarmac of the car park with a resounding clang and a huge cheer rang out from the spectators.

The Currie twins appeared by Hamish's side.

"Well, you're a man of your word, Hamish Macbeth," said Nessie. "No matter what anyone says, a man of your word."

"Man of your word," Jessie agreed and they marched off toward the village.

Bland looked at Hamish and laughed, then Colonel Halburton-Smythe pulled up in his Range Rover, lowering himself out of the cabin to marvel at the spectacle of the bridge, which was now swarming with soldiers attaching side rails and other finishing touches.

"A first-class job!" the colonel said, beaming with delight. "You can always trust the British Army to do a first-class job!"

"Aye," Hamish agreed, "and we can ay rely on Freddy to do a first-class job in your Tommel Castle kitchen. Those two officers and the gentleman wi' the beard will be joining Sergeant Bland and myself for the dinner you promised us, if that's all right with you."

"I…well…yes, of course," the colonel stammered. "That is what was agreed…more or less."

A party atmosphere broke out in the picnic area. Bottles of beer were thrust into soldiers' hands and drams of whisky in plastic cups were soon to follow. Hamish stepped forward to shake hands with Finlay and the Munro brothers, and invite them to dinner.

CHAPTER THREE

I cannot tell how the truth may be,
I say the tale as it was said to me.
Sir Walter Scott, *The Lay of the Last Minstrel*

"Hamish! There's somebody in the house!" The voice was hushed and quavering with fear, but there was no mistaking who it was.

"Angela," Hamish said, clamping the phone to his ear with his right hand and reaching for his trousers with the other. "Is Dr. Brodie no' at home?"

"No, he's out on an emergency up near Cromish. I'm here alone... at least, I was. There's somebody downstairs!"

"Lock yourself in the bathroom, Angela," Hamish said, struggling into his clothes. "I'll be right there."

He rushed out onto the landing, Lugs and Sonsie wisely keeping well out of his way, and hammered on James's door.

"James! Rouse yerself!" he yelled. "We got a call! Burglar on the premises!"

By the time he finished speaking he was thundering down

the stairs. He was in the Land Rover about to drive off when James piled into the passenger seat, pulling on his shirt.

"Where are we headed?" James said above the roar of the engine.

"Dr. Brodie's surgery. Angela's on her own and somebody's broken in!"

It took less than a minute to reach the short lane that led away from the loch up to where the doctor's house stood. Hamish left the car skewed across the end of the lane, blocking any getaway vehicle that might appear. They dashed to the house, ready to tackle a fearsome criminal, only to find Angela Brodie opening the front door.

"He's gone," she said slowly. "Ran out the back."

"Are you all right?" Hamish asked her as Bland headed round the house to check out the rear garden. "Did he hurt you?"

"No," she replied, a tear forcing its way onto her cheek. "I was so frightened..." She burst into tears and sobbed on Hamish's chest. He put a comforting arm round her, then saw Bland returning, shaking his head.

"Quiet now," he said softly to Angela. "Just listen, both of you."

"Can't hear a thing," Bland whispered.

"Exactly," Hamish said. "The bridge is the only way out of town. We'd easy hear a car or van engine. James, bide here wi' Angela."

Hamish ran back to the Land Rover and headed for the temporary bridge, blocking it with the car just as he had blocked the lane. He then stood for a few moments in the darkness of the picnic area, listening. Apart from the rush of the river and the more distant, rhythmic wash of waves on the beach, Lochdubh was wearing the night's darkness like a shroud of silence. He began walking slowly back toward the doctor's house, checking gardens, shining his torch into dark corners in the hope of flushing out his quarry. It was then that the moaning apparitions started to materialize. Shuffling along the pavement by the main road, some of them wore long, floating nightdresses, some were in tartan dressing gowns and others in pajamas so neatly pressed that Hamish suspected they had been hastily put on especially for this public appearance.

"Sergeant Macbeth! Someone's been in my house!"

"Hamish! We've been burgled!"

"He's made off wi' the electric money!"

Hamish quickly found himself addressing a clutch of Lochdubh residents, some brandishing pokers and cast-iron saucepans. They had been woken by the sound of his Land Rover speeding through the town, only to discover that they had played host to an uninvited nocturnal visitor. He held up his hands and appealed for calm.

"I know there's been someone sneaking around," he said, "but the best thing you can all do now is to go back home and take your pots, pans and fire irons wi' you. Lock your doors and windows and stay inside. We'll be scouring the area looking for the burglar. I'll be out to see all o' you in the morn."

He shooed them along the street as if he were herding ducks and watched each of them disappear back into their homes to the sound of turning locks, rattling chains and bolts being thrown. He then made his way back to the doctor's house, scanning every shadowy hiding place along the way with his torch. When he arrived, the front door was locked and when he knocked, Bland was the one who answered it.

"We're in the kitchen," Bland said. "That's where he got in."

"How's Angela?"

"She's a bit shaken up, but she's doing okay."

"There's been other break-ins. I've just had to deal wi' a gang o' vigilantes."

They made their way through to the back of the house where Angela greeted Hamish with a smile. She was leaning against a kitchen work surface cradling a glass of brandy, the bottle standing open on the counter.

"Any sign of him?" she asked.

"No' yet," Hamish replied.

"I reckon he reached in through the open toplight on this window," Bland said, indicating the window above the kitchen sink, "and managed to open the main window. There are muddy marks on the sink where he climbed in."

"It's no' a very big window," Hamish noted. "He'd need to be small and agile to climb through there. Did you get a look at him, Angela?"

"I saw him over there." Angela pointed past the open kitchen door across the hall to a door marked "Surgery." "He was trying to force the surgery door."

"Looking for any drugs he could find, no doubt." Hamish nodded. "Did you see his face?"

"The lights were out," Angela said, taking a deep breath to steady her voice. "I was on the stairs, phoning you. He turned and looked straight at me. He wasn't a bit afraid. He just smiled. He was wearing a hoodie but I could see him clearly by the light of his own torch. He had a gold tooth and blue eyes—that sort of cold blue, you know? Like a wolf."

"Did he threaten you at all?" Hamish asked.

"No, but he started coming toward me. It was then that I saw the tattoo on his neck—a spider's web. It reached right up onto his jaw. I ran upstairs and locked myself in the bathroom, like you told me to. I heard your car outside. He must have heard it, too, and he ran off, out the back door."

"You did the right thing, Angela," Hamish said, gently. "Now, let's get everything locked up here. James and I need to have a wee walk through the village to see if he's still around. Will you be okay on your own, or would you like me to get..."

"Mrs. Brodie!" The full-throated warble of Mrs. Wellington, the minister's wife, announced her imminent arrival at the front door which had been left ajar. "Are you all right? Are you hurt? I came as soon as I heard. Everyone's talking about this dreadful burglar."

Mrs. Wellington was a large woman dressed, as always, in a tweed jacket and skirt. Her dark hair was imperturbably set as hard as a crash helmet and her face was powdered and primped as if she were stepping out for lunch with ladies of the local Church of Scotland Guild rather than rushing to an incident in the middle of the night. There were, however, signs that she had prepared in haste. The buttons of her tweed jacket were in the wrong holes, creating a lopsided effect, and where her skirt ended, just below the knee, her legs were shockingly bare, lacking the robust stockings in which they were usually encased. The real giveaway, however, was her footwear. In place of her customary sensible, stout shoes were frivolously fluffy carpet slippers.

"Mrs. Wellington—just the person we need right now," Hamish said. "Angela's had an intruder. We have to lock up the house and scour the village for him. Would you bide here wi' Angela for a wee while, until she's settled?"

"Of course," Mrs. Wellington said, without hesitation. She crossed the room to where Angela stood, shoved the cork firmly back in the brandy bottle and took Angela by the arm. "Come along, my dear, let's get you back to bed."

Hamish and Bland swept the village but could find no trace of the man with the spider's web tattoo or any getaway car waiting hidden until the coast was clear. Eventually, they collected the Land Rover from the bridge and headed back to the station. Hamish sat down at his desk to compile an initial report, sending Bland off to bed.

"There's still time for a couple o' hours' shut-eye," he said. "I'll be doing the same myself afore long. I do some o' my best thinking just as I'm falling asleep."

He spent only a few minutes on the report before he, too, headed upstairs, heaving Lugs and Sonsie off the duvet in order to ease himself into bed. They were back within seconds and he reached out a hand to stroke Lugs's head. There were threads of thought drifting around in his mind, tangling themselves into a knot he knew could unravel if he could just pluck at the right thought.

There was something about the intruder that had struck a chord in his head, although he was sure it was nothing to do with the break-ins. Angela must have been terrified by the tattooed burglar with the wolf eyes. Where was it she had said Dr. Brodie had gone? Somewhere near Cromish. He sat up in bed. The tattoo—spiders—Cromish. Suddenly he knew who the young woman in the peace-camp photo was. He lowered his head back onto the pillow. With a bit of digging on the internet, he knew he could now shine a little more light on the shadowy spy ring.

Hamish was back at his computer the following morning when Bland came downstairs managing to yawn, stretch, pat Lugs and offer to make breakfast all at the same time. A few minutes later, with mugs of coffee and bacon sandwiches the size of house bricks on the table in front of them, both men sat down to eat.

"So what do you make of our disappearing burglar last night?" Bland asked.

"He didn't disappear," Hamish said, taking a mouthful of coffee. "He didn't drive out o' Lochdubh, so the way I see it, there's only three options. The first is that he walked out up into the hills."

"Possible, but tricky, even dangerous in the dark. Apart from falling off a cliff, I heard the peat bogs out there can suck you under and swallow you whole."

"Aye, that's true enough. And if he walked, he'd still be walking. It's a mighty hike to get anywhere from here on foot. The second option is that he sneaked out of town on a bicycle."

"Could be. We wouldn't have heard a pedal cycle escaping over the bridge. It's not a brilliant getaway vehicle, though, is it?"

"No, and our burglar is an opportunist—your basic, lazy sneak thief. He must have known full well that most folk around here never bother locking their back doors. Some never even lock the front door. So he went out in the middle o' the night looking for easy pickings. A lazy scunner like that is no' likely to be hiking or cycling through the hills around here."

"So what's your third option?"

"The third option is that he never left Lochdubh—he's still here."

"Wouldn't you know of anyone around here fitting that description?"

"Aye, he'd stick out like a kilt on a sheep, but there are a few holiday cottages around Lochdubh and the main season's near passed, so some of those will now be standing empty. He could be hiding out in one o' them. We also have a few strangers in town—the lads that Finlay sent to start work on the bridge."

"This burglar sounds pretty distinctive. He'd be easy to spot on a work detail."

"We can go down to the bridge this morning and take a look. If he's no' there, maybe somebody knows something about him. Seems like another one o' those coincidences, does it no'? A bunch o' lads show up in Lochdubh and there's a sudden spate o' burglaries."

"I guess we'll have to talk to everyone who got a visit from him last night."

"Aye, we'll get details from them afore lunch and then we can head down to see Lachlan at Lochcarron."

"That would be good. I hate to push you when you've got your hands full, but we need to keep moving forward with our list of spies."

"Well, I did a wee bit o' work on that earlier and I've some good news for you. I know where Alex Caldwell is."

Hamish took a bite from his bacon sandwich and began

chewing, a satisfied smile on his face betraying how pleased he was that he'd managed to achieve what Bland and his secret service chums, with all their resources, had failed to do. Bland leaned back in his chair, folding his arms and grinning, clearly amused at the way Hamish was eking out his moment of triumph.

"Come on, Hamish, spill the beans. I spent a lot of time trying to trace him. Where is he?"

"Would you mind showing me those photos you had o' the protestors at the peace camp?"

It took Bland only a few moments to retrieve the pictures from his room. Hamish finished off his sandwich and brushed crumbs off his hands onto his trouser legs before flicking through the photographs. He slid one across the table to Bland.

"That's Alex Caldwell," he said, tapping a finger on the photograph of the female protestor he had previously felt he recognized. "You were looking for a man, but Alex Caldwell is a woman.

"It was the spider's web tattoo and the mention o' Cromish that did it. When we were chasing Bogdan, the Russian who killed Morgan Mackay, we tracked him to a cottage on the outskirts o' Cromish, where he held this woman prisoner. She's young in that photo, but an old lady now—Moira Stephenson. She once phoned me because she was terrified by a plague o' the spiders in her house.

"We thought it was just her bad luck that Bogdan chose her house to rest and bandage his wounded leg, but maybe he knew exactly where he was going, because Moira was once part o' the network.

"I checked through records o' births, marriages and deaths, the electoral roll and suchlike, and she wasn't always Moira Stephenson. She was originally Moira Alexandra Black. I'm guessing she went by the name Alex Black because it seemed cool to her at the time. She then married Ian Caldwell but they divorced after ten years. She became Moira Stephenson when she remarried. Her second husband died twelve years ago."

"So she was Alex Caldwell when our list was compiled. That's good detective work, Sergeant Macbeth," Bland said. "The name changes over the years would have foxed me, even if I hadn't been concentrating on finding a man! We need to pay Mrs. Stephenson a visit."

"Aye, but no' just yet," Hamish said, taking a final gulp of coffee. "She was genuinely shocked and frightened last time I saw her. I think she's been out o' the game for a long time. If she's now been forced back in, then visiting her will let the others know we're closing in on them. It might even put her in danger."

"Okay, buddy, we'll do it your way. We still don't know what the remains of the Dozen are up to, so you're right, we need to tread softly. Let's get out and find out what our burglar got up to last night."

The two police officers worked their way, door-to-door, along the houses on the main street. Most of the residents had seen and heard nothing until the commotion caused by the police car racing through the village. Three had definitely fallen victim to the burglar. A watch and some jewelry had been taken from one house, a wallet from another. The wallet was subsequently found in the back garden. The credit cards, debit cards and driving license were still present; only the cash was missing. In the third house, Mr. and Mrs. Morrison were devastated that the jar they kept on their living-room mantelpiece, where they saved pound coins to pay their electricity bill, had been emptied.

"This is where Joe Donaldson lives," Hamish explained as they approached the last house before the doctor's surgery. "They call him 'Dribblin' Joe.'"

"Why's that?" Bland asked, laughing.

"Well, he's ay had one o' yon big flat-screen TVs—gets a bigger one every couple o' years. The screen's up on the wall and it lights up the whole living room. When you walk past in the street you can see him sitting there, sound asleep in front o' the telly, head on his chest, dribbling."

Hamish knocked once on the door but had no time for a second rap before it was flung open, Joe Donaldson standing before them. A retired engineer in his sixties, he was balding, overweight, and lived alone.

"Thank goodness you're here, Sergeant Macbeth!" he said, dramatically distressed. "This is a disaster! I'm at my wits' end!"

"Calm down, Joe," said Hamish, before introducing Bland. "Were you burgled last night?"

"Burgled?" wailed Donaldson. "Looted, more like! Pillaged! Come ben and I'll show you."

He led them into his comfortably furnished living room where everything seemed neat, tidy and in its proper place, apart from the large bare patch on the wall above the mantelpiece.

"Crivens, Joe, where's your TV?" said Hamish, reaching out to pat the wall next to the exposed cables that should have plugged into the back of the screen.

"That's it!" Donaldson said, wringing his hands. "That's what the bugger took! What am I going to do? I can't sit here all day staring at yon empty wall!"

"No, Joe," Hamish said slowly, leaning down slightly to look Donaldson straight in the eye. "I mean, *where* is your TV?"

"I...I mean...how should I know?" His eyes flicked toward the window that looked out over the back garden. "He took it..."

"Really?" Hamish took off his cap and made a show of scratching his head. "You see, the other things that have been stolen have been cash and jewelry, that sort o' thing. Small things, you know? Things that the burglar could easily slip into a pocket. Nothing as big as your seventy-five-inch screen. It must be just about time for you to get a new one, is it no'? I expect the latest ones are awfy expensive. It would be braw if your insurance company would fork out for a new one, would it no'?"

"I...umm, the thought never occurred," Donaldson stammered. "I...I've just had such a shock..."

"Well, now that the shock's worn off a wee bit, think hard, Joe," Hamish said. "Where is your TV?"

"Ah! Aye, that's it!" Donaldson's face lit up with a fair rendition of surprise and delight. "I took it down last night to clean behind it."

"Och, that explains it," Hamish said, slowly nodding, "and with all that talk about burglaries, you just panicked when you saw it missing and forgot you'd taken it down." He followed the track Donaldson's eyes had taken, glancing out the window to where a shed stood in the garden. "Out in the shed is it, Joe? It must have been a struggle for you to manhandle it on your own. Why don't Sergeant Bland and I go get it and put it back on the wall for you?"

"That…would be very kind of you, Sergeant Macbeth," Donaldson said, staring at the carpet, shamefaced.

Once they had rehung Dribblin' Joe's TV, Hamish and Bland walked together toward the bridge.

"You went kinda easy on that guy back there," Bland said. "No official reprimand, not even a harsh word."

"As far as I'm concerned," Hamish said, "that was crime prevention in operation. We prevented a crime—insurance fraud—from being committed."

"He's lucky that you were prepared to turn a blind eye."

"Aye, but what was in it for me? Yet more paperwork. He's no' a bad lad. He's certainly no' the first to try to scam his insurers and he'll no' be the last. Right now, however, he knows fine that I knew what he was up to. That means he'll be grateful and helpful in future."

"He owes you one."

"If you like, but no' in the way I owe you. I'll no' forget about that wee matter on the bridge the other night. That's twice you've saved my skin."

"Forget it," Bland said, waving a hand to dismiss the thought. "You'd have done the same for me."

"Aye, but that makes no odds. I'm still in your debt." He turned and looked in the direction of the bridge. "Right, let's get down to the river. We have to meet the foreman there—Stephanie Gibson. I suppose she'll be a forewoman, or is it a foreperson?"

"Site team manager," Bland said, grinning and waggling his smartphone. "I looked her up on the council website after Finlay mentioned her at dinner."

They walked down to where the road was redirected toward the army's temporary bridge, edged round the crush barriers and looked down to where the six-man council crew was at work. Although the Anstey had not yet returned to its normal level, the water was no longer threatening to overflow the banks and was not running as fast as it had been. A mechanical digger with a backhoe was scooping stones that had once been part of the bridge out of the water. Some of the workmen were manhandling the stones into neat piles according to size. The rest of the crew was dragging debris out from under the bridge. Two of the workmen looked up after settling a large stone on its pile. They leant together, talking softly to each other, their eyes never leaving the two police officers up near the road.

"What d'you think those two want?" the first man said.

"Who knows?" said his workmate, grinning. "What do the polis ever want? Maybe they've come to see what hard work looks like!"

"The lanky one is that Hamish Macbeth, is it no'?" The first man took off his work gloves. He was powerfully built and wiped the sweat of honest toil from his forehead with the back of a hand so big that it looked like it could do the job of the digger's scoop. "The other one looks weird."

"Must be that Yank we heard about in the pub last night."

The second man was slightly smaller, but had the wiry, muscular physique of a man used to heavy, manual labor. "They're calling the gaffer over."

The site team manager, a tall, slim woman with a mass of dark curly hair struggling to break free from beneath her yellow hard hat, strode toward Hamish and Bland, shook hands, identified herself as Stephanie Gibson, then nodded and waved to her crew to gather round. The digger driver climbed down from his cab and they all trudged up to find out what was going on. Once the six-man team had assembled, Hamish introduced himself and Bland.

"There was someone out in the village last night," he explained, "thieving from houses."

"So that's what this is about." The wiry workman let out a laugh. "There's been some burglaries and you want to pin them on one o' us because we're no' from round here."

There was muttering and grumbling from the other workmen.

"Not at all," Hamish responded. "We wanted to ask if any of you has seen a man wi' a spider's web tattoo on his neck. He also has distinctive blue eyes."

There was another murmuring and a shaking of heads.

"Your manager tells me that you're all staying at Mrs. Mackenzie's boarding house," Hamish said.

"All except me," said Stephanie. "Mrs. Mackenzie had no more rooms, so I'm at the Tommel Castle Hotel."

"It's all right for some, eh?" shouted the wiry workman, whose jibe was followed by a chorus of jeers, catcalls and laughter from her workforce.

"Shut it, you lot!" she said, smiling. "Sorry, Sergeant.

They're like a bunch o' bairns!" Her smile faded a little when she failed to catch Hamish's eye, and she looked down at her boots.

"Take care o' your valuables at night," Hamish warned the men. "It looks like the burglar is after jewelry, cash and the like."

"If I had any cash worth stealin', I wouldn't be stayin' in Mackenzie's shitehouse!" said one of the men before joining in the laughter of his friends.

"Just take care, lads," Hamish said, raising an open hand to motion for silence. "The suspect is probably still in the area. I don't want him getting his hands on your wages. If you see anybody answering the description, don't approach him, just let us know."

Stephanie sent the men back to work and, once they were out of earshot, Hamish turned to her once more.

"Any o' them have a criminal record?" he asked.

"That's not really for me to say, Sergeant," she said with a sigh, "but none of them even remotely fits the description of your burglar."

"That's not what I asked," Hamish said. "Has any of them been in trouble?"

"Well, he doesn't make any secret of it, and I suppose you'd find out anyway," she said, eventually. "Kevin, the digger driver, did time for breaking and entering, but he was released early, on parole—good behavior and all that."

Hamish watched Kevin heave himself back into his cab. He was a large man, bulky and overweight.

"Any of the others?" he asked again.

"Not that I know of," she said.

"How long will you be here in Lochdubh?" Hamish rummaged in a pocket for his notebook.

"We need to clear out all the debris that fell from the bridge as well as the stuff that the river brought down off the hill," the manager explained, "then try to shore up the riverbank in places where it's collapsed. We need the water to go down a bit for that. We've enough work here to keep my lads busy right up to when I take them out on the crew bus on Saturday around ten. On Monday, the engineers and construction team take over."

"None of your lads has his own transport?" Hamish asked.

"No, I brought them in and I'll be driving them out."

Hamish made a note of her phone number and she said goodbye in order to answer a call, looking back over her shoulder to give a smile and a wave as she headed for a table in the picnic area with her mobile clamped to her ear.

"Stephanie was real nice," Bland said, walking with Hamish back toward the village.

"Aye, very helpful," Hamish agreed.

"And she was a good-looking girl," Bland said, looking out over the loch, then glancing toward Hamish. "You can't say you didn't notice."

"Aye, she was pretty, right enough."

"Oh, come on, Hamish!" Bland laughed. "What about all those little looks and smiles? They were for you, not me. You can't have been totally oblivious to them. She had the hots for you, buddy!"

Bland thought he could see a slight flush of pink on

Hamish's cheek, but if he did, Hamish quickly disguised it by removing his cap, looking up to the hills and running his hand through his fiery red hair.

"That's all very well, but it's chust...No doubt she hass..." The sibilance in Hamish's Highland accent shone through when he was feeling uncomfortable. "I'm sure she'll have a boyfriend and...I also haff someone and...I haff no time for anything like that now."

"You're seeing someone?" Bland smiled. "You've never mentioned her."

"Aye, well, like I said," Hamish said, jamming his cap back on his head, "there's no time for all that right now. Come away now and we'll grab a coffee from Willie and Lucia afore we head down to Lochcarron. We need to talk to Mrs. Mackenzie later as well. She has seven rooms to rent, so someone else must be staying with her."

"We should also check out the Tommel Castle."

"I spoke to Silas earlier and there's no one staying there fits the description but it's ay a good idea to show the uniform and see if it makes anyone a bit nervous. We can drop by there tonight."

The Napoli, described by Willie Lamont as Lochdubh's finest Italian restaurant, conveniently ignoring the fact that there was no other such establishment in the village, was closed when they arrived, but Hamish led the way round to an area of decking by the kitchen door, where they were greeted by Lucia. With her waves of dark hair, her almond eyes and her voluptuous figure, she had been compared by some to a young Gina Lollobrigida. Hamish wasn't entirely sure who that was, save that she had been a film star during Hollywood's most glamorous era, but, given that Lucia was undoubtedly beautiful, he had always assumed the comparison to be valid. Quite what Lucia had seen in plain old Willie Lamont, Hamish had never understood, but love, so they say, is blind and the two seemed blissfully happy together running the Napoli. She took a break from working in the kitchen to join Hamish and James in the morning sunshine at a little table by the kitchen door. Willie fussed over them all, cleaning the table and chairs, as was his obsession, and serving them coffee.

"I loved your food when we were here on the night of the storm," Bland said.

"*Grazie*, Mr. Bland," Lucia said, with a glorious smile. "I am so liking it here when the weather is sunny like today, but with the cold and wind and rain, no' so much."

Hamish had always been charmed by her accent, a delightfully soft mix of Italian and Scottish.

"No doubt we'll be back in again afore James has to head home," he said, sipping his coffee.

"Maybe no' the night, though, Hamish," Willie said, finally sitting down to join them. "We've a wedding party coming in by coach from Braikie. They're having the reception here after they've been to a wee chapel in the hills for the rupturals."

"Nuptials, I think, Willie," Hamish corrected him.

They chatted for a few minutes before the two police officers made their way back to the station to pick up the car for their drive south.

"Make sure you lock up good and proper at night now," Hamish warned Willie quietly as they left, taking care not to alarm Lucia. "We don't want you getting a visit from the tattooed burglar."

* * *

A little more than two hours later, having motored down past Ullapool and along the shores of Loch Broom and Loch Glascarnoch to join the A832 heading southwest to Loch Carron, they were approaching their destination. Sitting in the passenger seat, Bland gazed out the window at the latest in a long list of lochs and lochans strung out along their route.

"Loch Doughaill," Bland said, studying the road map on his lap rather than the car's satnav screen. "Does the name mean something?"

"You could take it to mean 'Loch o' the Dark Stranger,'" Hamish said, his eyes never leaving the winding road. "That's a possible translation into English."

"Sounds intriguing. Is there some sort of legend associated with it?"

"There's ay a legend or myth o' some kind," Hamish said with a mischievous smile, "and if there's no', you can ay make one up! The name's likely linked to the MacDowell or MacDougall clans and it's a bonny wee loch wi' yon steep slopes rising off the far shore. Loch Carron's a bit more interesting. That's the 'Loch o' Rough Water.' Doughaill's a wee inland loch, but Carron opens out onto the Inner Sound and the North Atlantic. A fisherman I know told me Loch Carron's more than three hundred feet deep in places and the Inner Sound can be well over a thousand. They say it's the deepest water anywhere in the UK."

"That's deeper than Chicago's Lake Michigan."

"Aye, but you could empty every loch in Scotland and still no' fill Lake Michigan—I've read a fair bit about where you come from."

"You been checking up on me, Hamish?" Bland gave a little laugh.

"Aye, I have that," Hamish said, briefly looking across at his passenger. "Don't forget that the last time you were here I had you down as a murder suspect."

"Yeah, I remember," Bland said, folding the map, "but murder's not my business."

"Maybe one day," Hamish grunted, "I'll work out just what your business really is. Looks like we're coming into Lochcarron."

The roadside trees gave way to a gently undulating expanse of open moorland that seemed to push the hills further from the road. They passed a clutch of buildings including a wooden lodge offering bed and breakfast, a café and a craft center before they reached the church and graveyard that marks the periphery of so many settlements in the Highlands. Loch Carron's dark waters began to dominate their view to the left and the low, white buildings of the local primary school appeared on their right. The Lochcarron Hotel then announced a procession of cottages and houses, either white-painted or with rough stone walls, strung out along the loch. Only the road and a narrow pavement separated the buildings from the foreshore.

When the road swung away from the loch and houses crowded either side, they came across Loch Carron police station on their left. The modern white station house and its attached office looked little different to the nearby homes and might easily have been mistaken for one of them. The station house was, of course, home to its resident officers, but the police sign and the patrol car parked in the driveway betrayed its alternate purpose. Hamish parked in the bay in front of the station and had no sooner switched off the engine than a burly, bearded, balding police officer came bustling out to greet them.

"Hamish!" he cried, his handshake swiftly turning into a bear hug. "It's grand to see you again, laddie!"

"Lachlan, this is James Bland," Hamish said, and Lachlan offered Bland a warm greeting. "James is here from Chicago taking a look at how we do things on this side o' the pond."

Hamish felt bad about having to lie to his friend but saw no point in dragging Lachlan in to the murky world of spies and traitors.

"Come ben, now," Lachlan said, leading the way into the station. "I'm just after putting the kettle on."

A few moments later, Hamish and Bland were seated around a small table in a clean and airy modern kitchen, each with a mug of tea in front of him. Lachlan placed a plate of short-bread biscuits on the table, some of them chocolate coated.

"There's a wee woman lives just up the road makes these," he said, helping himself. "She ay brings some by when she's baked a batch. She knows I can't resist the chocolate ones!"

Lachlan was keen to enjoy a catch-up with Hamish, their chat revolving around mutual friends and the Anstey Bridge Disaster, news of which had spread throughout the region faster than a flicker of summer lightning.

"And I'm awful glad to see you looking so well," Lachlan laughed, "because, by the time the story reached me, it had you being dragged out o' a submerged van, barely alive!"

"It wasn't quite as bad as all that," Hamish said. "These

stories ay get a wee bit more entertaining wi' each telling. Now, what we want to hear about from you is the car that went into the Inner Sound out near Applecross a few weeks back."

"Aye, that was an awfy business," Lachlan said, gravely. "After they recovered the body, the pathologist said he had seawater in his lungs, so he was alive when the car went into the water."

"He lived locally, didn't he?" asked Bland.

"He did that," Lachlan confirmed, "but he ay traveled a lot. He was a music teacher—piano mainly—and he visited schools far and wide. All the way down to Fort William, even Oban. What's your interest in him?"

"We're trying to track down a missing person," Hamish said, the lie coming easily with it being basically true—they were trying to track down several missing persons.

"Maybe there's someone local we could talk to about the dead man?" Bland asked.

"Callum Graham," Hamish said, looking at his notes, even though he had memorized the name, somehow expecting that a new revelation about the man might leap out of the page. "Did he have relatives living nearby?"

"His only relative was his niece, Jean Graham, who runs a wee bed and breakfast place up near Shieldaig," replied Lachlan. "Her uncle took her in after her parents died—one wi' the cancer and one wi' a heart attack—when she was just a bairn. I had to break the news to her about her uncle. She was awfy upset."

"I guess that's understandable," said Bland. "It hits people hard when they lose someone that close."

"Aye, but it wasn't just that," Lachlan said, a dramatic tone in his voice. "She had no doubt in her mind that this was no accident. She claims her uncle was murdered!"

"Actually, we were kind of thinking the same thing," Bland said.

"That's as may be," Lachlan said, slowly, "but she claimed she had a visit from someone in the middle o' the night who warned her to keep her trap shut or she'd end up at the bottom o' the Sound—and now she's gone missing!"

CHAPTER FOUR

Nae man can tether time or tide.
Robert Burns, "Tam o' Shanter"

In the Jacobite you could be forgiven for thinking that time
had stood still. Maybe not for the three centuries it had been
serving ale and whisky—there were, after all, electric lights
casting a feeble glow that failed to reach the inn's gloomiest
corners and music speakers leaking watery versions of last
century's greatest hits into the atmosphere—but Jacobite
time could certainly stand still for a few hours. In its darkest
alcoves, far from the nearest of the building's small windows, it
was impossible to tell if it was beer-with-lunch time, just-one-
last-beer time, or time to hit the road. The two men huddled
together in their customary corner, however, were very much
conscious of time—acutely aware that theirs was in danger of
running out.

"Well, that did us no good at all, did it?" said the first man.

"We got yon photos. That's bound to help, is it no'?" his
companion answered.

"Maybe, but we can't even be sure those are photos o' the right place! The boss is goin' to go mental. 'Get the truth out o' her,' is what he said. And what have we come up wi'? A couple o' holiday snaps."

"It's no' our fault that she wasn't there. I'll tell you, though, I had the weirdest feelin' that we were bein' watched. She wasn't in the house, but she wasn't far away, either."

"She's just like yon Graham woman. Now there's two o' them have vanished, as well as McGill."

"We should tell the boss we think she was watchin' us at the house."

"In the name o' the wee man! Have gone off your heid? If we tell him she's sneakin' about keepin' tabs on us, especially after we scared off Jean Graham, he'll be thinking we've turned into a right liability and that's no' goin' to end well for us, is it?"

"So what do we do now? Maybe the boss can identify the place in the photos, but he's banned us from goin' anywhere near him and he says we can't send anythin' to him in case his phones or his computer are tapped."

"Leave it wi' me. I'll set up another meet."

"His meetings give me the creeps. They're ay out in the middle o' nowhere in the middle o' the night."

"That's how he wants it. Away from people. Away from street cameras or any o' yon fancy doorbell cameras."

"I'm getting' right sick o' this!"

"Keep your heid! We'll be done wi' it all soon."

"Aye, right. You say that, but we're ay bein' dragged in deeper, and if we can't find this auld fool, we're dead men walking!"

*   *   *

Hamish and Bland left Lachlan dealing with a small, middle-aged local woman who had marched into the police station to complain about her noisy neighbors, who had been partying late into the night or, as she put it, "hoochin' an' choochin' till the sun rose!" They drove out of Lochcarron to find a narrow, single-track road that climbed into the mountains on the Applecross peninsula through a tortuous series of hairpin bends. This was the infamous Bealach na Bà, or Pass of the Cattle, an old drovers' route that was known to be one of the most challenging roads in Britain.

"If you were going to drive off a road," Bland commented, steadying himself with one hand on the dashboard as the Land Rover swung round the tightest of bends into a dauntingly steep climb, "this road would give you all the help you needed."

"Aye, but according to Lachlan, Graham knew these roads well," Hamish replied. "He had a good car and fair weather. This road's no' any good for motor homes or heavy trucks, but normal cars can manage it no bother if the drivers know what they're doing."

Within a few minutes, they were on the high moors and starting to descend. There were longer, straighter sections of road with views down to the Inner Sound and Raasay with the mountains of Skye beyond. On reaching the small fishing settlement of Applecross, they headed north along the shore road.

"So is there some kind of orchard here?" Bland asked, eyeing the name "Applecross" on the map lying in his lap.

"No, there's no' any orchard," Hamish replied. "There's

no' really much here at all. There's an inn, a shop, a few houses and that's about it. The locals don't even call the place Applecross—they just call it 'the Street.'"

"Where does the name come from, then?"

"It's a jumble o' Gaelic, maybe even Pictish words that basically mean the place is at the mouth of the River Crossan. It empties into the wee bay here. We need to head further up the coast to find the spot where Lachlan said the car went off the cliff."

There was no missing the site of the accident. A large area between the road and the cliff edge was still enclosed by blue-and-white police tape. Hamish drove on, rounding a bend to one of the many passing places spaced out along the road. He parked the Land Rover and they walked back, stepping over the tape barrier to examine the crash scene. Bland stumbled on a boulder hidden in the heather and Hamish caught his arm.

"It's a wee bit strange, is it no'?" he said. "This patch o' ground is near as lumpy as Mackenzie's boarding house beds. Even if you dozed off at the wheel, you'd be awake quick enough once you bounced into this stuff."

"It's an interesting spot as well," Bland added, looking back at the road. "The way the road bends, if you're coming from the south, you can't see this short stretch. Same if you're coming from the north."

They walked a few paces more to take a look over the cliff edge at the rocks below. Bland was surprised to see the car still there.

"They'll have recovered the body by boat, or maybe the mountain rescue lads brought him up the cliff here," Hamish said, "but recovering the car's a different story. It's no' easy to get the right sort o' crane up here by road. They might be waiting for a boat wi' lifting gear."

"Won't there be evidence in the car that might be destroyed by the water?"

"Evidence o' what? It's already been decided that this was an accident, remember. Graham lost control o' the car and drove off the cliff—that's the official story. There's no' any team o' detectives conducting an investigation."

"Except for us," Bland said, turning to walk the short distance back up to the road. "If Graham was murdered, then this is a pretty good spot for someone to have ambushed him—but there's no space to draw alongside and run him off the road. If someone wanted to get him, they'd have to make him stop. How do you stop a man in a car?"

"Flag him down," Hamish suggested. "Act like you're in trouble. Maybe even stage an accident."

"It's risky, though." Bland looked up and down the road. "I know this is a quiet road, but you can't see far to the north or south. Anybody could drive round one of those bends and catch you red-handed."

"Aye," Hamish agreed, looking up the hill, "so you'd want to post a lookout. Let's have a wee keek from up there."

They followed a time-worn rabbit-run path up through the heather until they reached a spot on the hillside where they could see the accident site below and the road beyond the bends.

"From up here," Hamish said, standing on a rock, "you could see a car coming from miles away in either direction."

"Then you signal to your guy down below to let him know

the target is approaching," Bland said, nodding. "But it's dark. How do you know you've got the right car?"

"You'd need someone back down the road, where it leaves the Street. A quick phone call is all it would take to let you know the right car was on its way. There's no other way to join this road."

"So we're talking about an accomplice back in the Street and an ambush team up here of two men," Bland reasoned.

"Three men," came a voice from behind them. "There were three men up here."

Hamish looked up to see a woman standing on a rocky outcrop about ten feet above them on the slope. She looked to be in her mid-thirties and well equipped for the outdoors with walking boots, hiking gear, a rucksack and a stout "cromach" walking staff.

"And who might you be?" he asked.

"I could ask you the same question," she replied. "You look like a policeman but I'm no' so sure about your sidekick."

"I'm Sergeant Hamish Macbeth," Hamish explained, "and this is my American colleague, Sergeant James Bland. Now it's your turn—who are you?"

"My name is Jean Graham."

"My pal Lachlan says you've gone missing."

"Well, you can tell your pal that I'm no' missing. I just don't want to be found. There's a difference."

"Jean, we'd like to talk to you about your uncle," said Bland, taking a step higher on the slope.

"You bide right where you are!" She hefted the cromach, waving its heavy, gnarled head at Bland. "You'll no' be talking to anyone about anything after a skelp in the heid wi' this."

"All right, Jean," Hamish said, gently tugging Bland's sleeve to draw him back. "We can talk from here. What makes you think your uncle's death was more than an accident?"

"Accident?" Jean scoffed. "It was no accident. He ay warned me that something might happen to him and told me that, if it did, I should make myself scarce."

"Why do you think he believed he might be in danger?" asked Bland.

"I don't know for sure," Jean said, planting the bottom of her cromach back on the ground while still keeping a wary eye on Bland. "I ay thought it might be the gambling. Over the years, he sometimes mentioned other people in a way that made them sound like some kind o' gang. I thought maybe he owed them money."

"What was he doing up here the night it happened?" asked Hamish.

"He often drove this road. Sometimes he'd come all the way round the coast road after visiting me in Shieldaig. He'd stop at a place just north of here at Sand. He'd sit there for ages at night, staring at the stars."

"You said you thought there were three men," Bland said. "Why's that?"

"There was one up here, keeping watch," she said. "He stood here on this rock. I can feel him here. I know this is where he stood, looking down, watching Uncle Callum being murdered. Down on the road, you'd need two men to be sure of overpowering him and to send his car over the cliff. I've sat here many times since he was killed and, in my mind's eye, I can see it all."

"Do the names William McAllister, James Smith or John

Martin mean anything to you?" Hamish asked. "Did your uncle ever mention them?"

"Why? Are they the three who killed them?" Jean demanded.

"They're three men we're trying to trace," Bland explained. "They might be able to shed some light on what happened to your uncle."

"Then I hope you find them," Jean said, "but I've never heard o' them."

"Jean, come wi' us, lassie," Hamish offered. "We'll keep you safe. You can trust us."

"Trust you?" Jean gave a snort. "That'll be the day. I've had strangers threatening me because I was telling whoever would listen that my uncle was murdered. I can't trust anyone right now. I can't trust a soul until you find who killed Uncle Callum. I'm better off on my own. I know every bothy, dun, cave and abandoned croft in these hills and I've food stashed in a dozen places. I can survive up here for weeks and neither you nor them will ever find me!"

"I can't let you do that, Jean," Hamish said, making to climb up toward her. She lifted her cromach again.

"Stay back!" she snarled. "You might look like cops but I'm no' takin' any chances! Carol told me she had two dodgy blokes come to her, looking for her father. That could be you two!"

"Carol?" Bland said with a frown. "Would that be Carol McGill, Dennis McGill's daughter? Your uncle and Dennis were friends, weren't they?"

"Aye, Carol and I were pretty much brought up together. I lost my mum and dad within a couple o' years o' each other when I was just a bairn. Carol's like a sister to me. Her dad's made himself scarce and she's keeping her heid down now as well."

"It's a dangerous game that you and the McGills are playing," Hamish told her. "You need to come wi' us."

"No way!" Jean shouted, then laughed. "And you'll no' be going anywhere for a while anyway. Here—catch!"

She threw something small and metallic to Hamish, who plucked it out of the air.

"Yon's the locking wheel nut from one o' your Land Rover's back wheels. You really should lock your car when you leave it, you know. The rest o' the nuts are hidden. Give me your phone number and a half-hour start. Don't try to come after me or I'll never tell you where to find the wheel nuts and you'll be stuck here for hours until you can get someone to come out here."

Jean keyed Hamish's number into her phone as he recited it, then she turned and headed off into the mountains, leaving Hamish and Bland to make their way back to the police car and await her call.

"Jean Graham was quite something," Bland said, standing by the car and looking up at the hillside.

"Aye, she was that," Hamish agreed, eyeing the Land Rover's toolbox that was sitting, open, by the rear wheel. The wheel was still on the car, but the wheel nuts were missing, just as Jean had promised. "I pity any o' the spy network who catches up wi' her and her cromach!"

Jean Graham was as good as her word, phoning in half an hour to let Hamish know that his wheel nuts were hidden in the heather on the opposite side of the road, near a gray rock. Once the wheel was firmly reattached to the car, they set off northward to find the parking spot Jean had described at Sand. From there they could look down on the small bay and the dunes after which the place was named. On the high ground to the left of the beach were caves and rock dwellings where archeologists had found evidence of settlers from more than 9,500 years ago. To the right was a more recent habitation. Hamish stared down at the small, gated access road; the anonymous, low, whitewashed buildings; and the discreet helicopter landing pad.

"That's the Royal Navy place, is it no'?" he said.

"Yeah, I'm guessing that stars weren't always the only thing he came here to see," said Bland. "Those buildings are BUTEC—the British Underwater Test and Evaluation Centre. It's now run by a private company but they work with your Ministry of Defense to test torpedoes, sonar and all sorts of other stuff out there in the Inner Sound."

"Suddenly," Hamish said, turning to look Bland in the eye, "you know an awfy lot about what goes on around these parts."

"I remember once telling you," Bland said with a thin smile, "that there's plenty goes on in your neck of the woods that's of interest to my employers. This is an important part of the world for us. It's not just that test facility down there. We now have more U.S. submarines operating off Europe than ever before, and they make plenty of stops at Faslane. Scotland, especially the Atlantic coast, is someplace we want to keep safe."

"So any remnants o' an auld spy ring need to be rooted

out," Hamish nodded, narrowing his eyes. "Rooted out and eliminated."

"Whoa, I see where you're going with this, buddy," Bland said, holding his hands up in front of him defensively, as though to keep Hamish at bay. "I'm not here to kill anyone. I don't want any more dead bodies showing up. I want these guys alive and happy to talk to us. We need to learn all we can about what they were up to and who else might be involved. We can't get a thing from a corpse."

"Except, perhaps, evidence that identifies the murderer," Hamish pointed out. He turned to climb back into the Land Rover. "Let's try to make sure there are no more killings. We need to get up to Thurso to track down McGill and his daughter. We can start by talking to his former employer."

"Are we heading there now?" Bland asked, hurrying round to the passenger door.

"No, it's a good four hours from here. We'll head back to Lochdubh. I need to check out the holiday homes, caravans and suchlike close to the village that might be standing empty. I still have a burglar to find." He started the engine and headed south, back to the mountain pass and Lochcarron.

"I'll get us an appointment to see someone at Dounreay," Bland said, fishing out his phone.

"Aye, you do that," Hamish said, a note of irritation in his voice. The thought of the trek all the way to Thurso was drawing a heavy black curtain across his mind. How could he concentrate on catching the burglar who was stalking the night in Lochdubh when he had all of this skulduggery with Bland pulling him away from his patch? And after Thurso they still had to talk to Daviot and Jimmy Anderson in Strathbane, not to mention the despicable Blair down in Glasgow. The trip to Glasgow alone would take a whole day—another day lost to the spies and traitors. How long was it going to be before he could get back to normal and start settling in for the Lochdubh winter that was just round the corner? He glanced across at Bland, who was deep into an animated phone conversation. If the American had noticed the dark temperament settling over his driver, then he was choosing to ignore it. Hamish sighed and concentrated on the road.

"Nobody who knew or worked with McGill at Dounreay is around at the moment," Bland announced, "but one of his old managers will be there on Friday."

"Fine," Hamish grunted. "Let's get to Strathbane early tomorrow to talk to Daviot and Jimmy," he continued. "Then we can carry right on down to Glasgow to see Blair. It's a long haul but we can share the driving and get it all done in a day."

On the way into Lochdubh, Hamish stopped at a number of different holiday-let cottages and crofts here and there where a corner of a field had been given over to caravan accommodation. Bland cheerfully lent a hand when it came to chatting with anyone they came across, to the extent that Hamish began to feel guilty about having sunk into such a sullen mood. Most of the places they visited were empty, locked up and secure, with no signs of anyone having taken up residence illicitly. At the final cottage, they encountered one family at the end of their holiday, weary from a day's hillwalking. The parents were downhearted at the thought of heading home to the daily grind of household chores and the stresses of work.

The teenaged children were far more enthusiastic about the forthcoming journey, looking forward to being reunited with all of the electronic internet gadgetry they had not been allowed to bring with them. Like everyone else they spoke to, however, the family had seen no sign of the tattooed burglar.

A few minutes later, they crossed the army's bridge and were driving along Lochdubh's waterfront. Hamish felt his mood lighten as soon as he saw the welcoming cottages nestling on the shore of the loch and the mountains standing tall, framing a vista that was so close to his heart. The clouds had yet to gather into heavy enough formations to blanket the mountain tops, failing to subdue the determined buoyancy of the dipping sun's early evening light. He spotted a familiar figure leaning on the harbor wall. Local fisherman Archie Maclean was deftly rolling a cigarette, defying the onshore breeze to pop it into his toothless mouth and light it with an ancient Zippo.

"There's a man who might be able to tell us about tattoos," Hamish announced, pulling over beside Archie, whose baggy sweatshirt and voluminous jeans flapped in the breeze when he turned on hearing the car.

"Does that old guy have an even older brother?" asked Bland. "Looks like he's wearing a much bigger guy's clothes."

"Archie's a fisherman," Hamish explained, "and his wife's an obsessive cleaner—even more than Willie at the Napoli. She hated the smell o' fish and cigarettes on his clothes, so she used to boil them in an auld copper cauldron. Actually, she used to boil pretty much everything in there. The thing was, she shrank all Archie's clothes so much he looked like he was wearing stuff he'd had since he was a bairn. Everything was tight as a haggis skin. Then he came into some money, bought her a brand-new washing machine and himself the baggiest breeks and shirts you've ever seen."

They joined Archie at the wall and he greeted them both with a cheery wave of his cigarette.

"I thought you'd given up, Archie," Hamish said, catching a fragrant whiff of tobacco smoke. Having once been a smoker himself, he still savored the smell, although he detested the candy-floss scents in the wet clouds emanating from tourists vaping on e-cigarettes.

"Aye, I've given up all right," Archie replied, nodding and smiling. "Given up at home, given up in the pub since they banned it, given up everywhere except on my boat or down here by the water. See yon selkie out there?" He pointed to an area of water where there was nothing to see, then took a drag on his cigarette only for a seal's head to appear on the loch. "He was ay a good smoker. He comes in to enjoy an evening smoke wi' me."

Bland gave Hamish a quizzical look and Hamish responded with an almost imperceptible shake of his head. At some point he would explain to the American that certain folk in the far northwest of Scotland firmly believed in witches, fairies and a select elite of supernatural creatures. Foremost among those convictions was the notion that the dead could return to enjoy the freedom of the seas in the afterlife as seals.

"I'll bet he does just that, Archie," Hamish said, going on to introduce Bland.

"I done heard y'all was back in town," Archie said, having watched enough old cowboy movies to make him think he

knew how Americans spoke. "I mind o' you bein' here afore."
His stab at an American accent didn't last long.

"And I loved it so much I just couldn't stay away," Bland
said, smiling.

"Archie, you'll have heard about this burglar, have you no'?"
Hamish asked.

"Folk around here are talking about nothing else," Archie
confirmed.

"So maybe you know he has a tattoo," Hamish said. "A
spider's web on his neck. Have you any tattoos yourself, you
being a sailor, after all?"

"None," Archie said, abruptly.

"Strike one," Bland said, laughing. "Hamish thought you
might know about tattoos, Archie. They're real fashionable
now—not just for sailors. Did you never want to have one
inked?"

"No," Archie said, then looked from Bland to Hamish and
back again, clearly realizing that they were expecting an expla-
nation. "When I first joined the merchant navy as a young laddie, my mother told me that if I ever came home wi' a tattoo,
she'd kick my arse so hard I'd be wearing it for a bonnet."

Archie gave a little chuckle, the other two taking that as
permission to laugh.

"I knew plenty as had the tattoos done," he went on, "and
yon spider's web can mean something or nothing. The man
you'd best ask about it is a man who has a tattoo himself. You
know him well, Hamish."

"I do?" Hamish was perplexed.

"Aye—the seer."

"No' Angus Macdonald, surely? That charlatan has a tattoo? Actually, why am I surprised?"

"Who is Angus Macdonald?" asked Bland.

"He takes money off people for telling fortunes, giving 'readings' and all sorts o' cons," Hamish explained. "I've had a mind to arrest him a few times for ripping people off, but his 'clients' won't hear a word said against the auld fraudster."

"The seer kens things, Hamish," Archie said, before taking a long drag on his cigarette. "He sees things. He kens things that have happened and things that have yet to happen. He's been useful to you in the past."

"Aye, you're right, Archie," Hamish agreed, patting the old man on the shoulder to make up for his tirade against the seer. "He knows plenty o' things. He picks up all the gossip from around here. There's no' much happens that he doesn't get to hear about. We should pay him a visit."

"You must take an offering," Archie reminded him.

"Aye, we'll do that," Hamish said, before bidding Archie farewell and getting back into the Land Rover.

"The seer sounds fascinating," Bland said, "but you think he's a con artist?"

"That I do," Hamish said, smiling and shaking his head, "but he's a grand source o' information. We can't visit him empty-handed, though. Let's stop at the Patels' shop and pick up something for him."

Angus Macdonald's cottage stood on an elevated grassy ledge that looked down on most of the rest of the village. Hamish had often thought that, from this vantage point, the seer could observe anything that was happening in Lochdubh. If someone had been hanging out washing on a

Sunday—something that was frowned upon by many of the staunchest churchgoers in the community—or had been restocking a peat store, or had been clearing leaves from their gutters, Macdonald would surely know about it. Weaving little tidbits like that into his "readings" or "predictions" was an ideal way, in Hamish's opinion, of pulling the wool over people's eyes.

Leaving the car down on the road, they walked up the narrow track that led to Macdonald's cottage. Hamish hesitated before knocking on the front door, wondering if what remained of the peeling paint would simply turn to dust and fall off if he rapped too hard. He needn't have worried. Before he could touch the door it swung open and the seer stood there, framed by the dark interior of his home. He had long, straggly white hair with an equally straggly white beard and was dressed in a floor-length white robe, a string of black beads draped around his neck. Judging by the way the robe bulged and the beads bunched on his podgy belly, he had put on weight since Hamish last saw him, and Macdonald had never boasted anything less than a rotund figure.

"The fortune-telling business must be booming, Angus," Hamish said, looking down at the smaller man's stomach. "You've no' been missing many meals."

"Welcome, Macbeth," Macdonald said, fixing Hamish with a look of cold disapproval in his soft gray eyes. He waved a hand toward his living room. "Come away ben."

"This is Sergeant—" Hamish began to introduce Bland but was cut short by Macdonald.

"I ken fine who this American is," Macdonald said, "although he is a man with many faces."

"We brought you this," Bland said, offering Macdonald a bottle of whisky.

"So you did," Macdonald said, examining the bottle with an appraising eye. "The Famous Grouse. A fine blend. No' as desirable as a single malt...no' as expensive, either." He accepted the gift without thanks and the whisky was spirited away into a cupboard.

They sat in wooden chairs by the fire, the sweet smell of burning peat permeating the room.

"Ask what you may," Macdonald said with a theatrical wave of his arm.

"Do you have a tattoo?" Hamish asked.

"I do," Macdonald replied, rolling up his sleeve. "This is identical to the one the great Sean Connery had."

"No, it's no'," Hamish said, examining the inked image of a bleeding heart with a dagger plunged vertically through it. It was the wording that concerned him. "Sean Connery's tattoo said, 'Scotland Forever.' Was your tattooist on the booze, because yours says 'Scotland Porker'?"

"Havers!" Macdonald grumbled, swiftly brushing his sleeve down. "It's just the way the design works and the light in here."

"Can you tell us anything about tattoos and what they mean?" asked Bland. "We're specifically interested in a spider's web tattoo on the neck of a suspect."

"There are many interpretations of the web design," Macdonald said, sitting back in his chair. "The ancient peoples where you come from saw the web as a shield, protecting them from harm. The spider woman is a powerful goddess in some Native American tribes. She spins a web over the cradles of newborn bairns to protect them from evil.

"In other societies, the web can be seen as a symbol of struggle. Just as the spider's prey struggles to escape, so must we struggle through life. This struggle is particularly important for those who have spent time in prison—unable to escape and struggling to survive until they can be free."

"So our guy might be a jailbird," said Bland.

"That doesn't really give us much to go on," Hamish said. "Can you tell us anything else you might have heard about the burglaries, Angus?"

"Only that the man you seek mocks you," Macdonald said, closing his eyes as though concentrating hard. "He believes he can do as he will. You may see him but not find him, and find him but not see him."

"Aye, right," Hamish said, running his hand through his hair. "That's about as much sense as I usually get from you. Come on, James. We should have a word wi' Mrs. Mackenzie, then get up to the hotel to talk to Silas."

Mrs. Mackenzie's boarding house was often described as warm, welcoming, comfortable and clean, with every modern convenience…but only by herself. Her sales pitch when prospective guests phoned to make an inquiry was delivered in a voice more polished than any of her second-hand furniture, and those who arrived expecting the accommodation to live up to her hyperbole very quickly decided to dig a little deeper into their pockets for a more expensive room at the nearby Tommel Castle Hotel.

Yet there were many holidaymakers who came back year after year, unable to resist the lure of Mrs. Mackenzie's bargain rates. The place was popular with hillwalkers and climbers, who were happy with her rudimentary rooms and rock-bottom prices. Outside the holiday season, she could always rely on steady trade from forestry workers, road menders and, following the recent storm, bridge builders. When Hamish and Bland pulled up, they could see her sitting in her front room, where guests were not allowed, engrossed in a dog-eared copy of *The People's Friend*. She scowled out the window at them when Hamish knocked on the front door.

"What do you want?" she demanded on opening the door. "I'm awfy busy right now."

She patted her hair as though settling curls that may have sprung out of place due to the effort she had been putting into some strenuously hard work. She was a small, round woman with a small round face and large pink glasses that clashed alarmingly with the violet hair rinse she applied once a week to color her grayness.

"We wanted to ask you about the guests you have with you at the moment," Hamish explained. "You have the six lads working at the bridge, I believe."

"I do," she nodded, folding her arms defensively over her ample bosom, "and a right pain they are. They're down the pub every night and come in here roaring drunk. I've warned them to get in afore ten o'clock, otherwise they'll be locked out."

"Who's staying in your other bedroom?" asked Bland.

"That's the big room out the back," she replied. "There's a nice young couple sharing the room—husband and wife." She emphasized the last phrase with a slow nod to make sure they understood she would never tolerate an unmarried couple sharing a room under her roof. "They're out walking in the hills most o' the day. They ay let me know what time they'll be back and pay extra for me to lay on a decent supper."

Hamish shuddered at the thought of what Mrs. Mackenzie would consider "a decent supper."

"And afore you ask," she went on, "neither o' them has any kind o' spidery tattoo. I've heard all about this burglar you're looking for, and you'll no' find him in my house."

"How long are they staying with you?" Hamish asked.

"They're here for another week—until next Wednesday."

"We'll be wanting to talk to them," Hamish informed her, handing her a card. "Just to ask if they've seen anyone suspicious while they've been out and about. Give them this please, and ask them to call me."

Mrs. Mackenzie viewed the card suspiciously but accepted it and disappeared back indoors. By the time Hamish and Bland were back in the Land Rover, she was back in her front room with her *People's Friend*.

"If we discount big Kevin the digger driver, who would never have fitted through the Brodies' kitchen window, then there are still six men at Mackenzie's place who could be our burglar," Hamish said, pulling away from the boarding house in the direction of the Tommel Castle Hotel.

"Except that none of them fits the description," Bland pointed out.

"No," Hamish said, shaking his head, "and that's really bothering me. Nobody living in the area fits the description, so he has to be an outsider, but there's nothing gets past the folk in Lochdubh. If there was someone staying anywhere near here who looked like our burglar, somebody would know about it."

"Maybe he's gone," Bland suggested. "With the army bridge in place, he could have left by now."

"No...he's still here. I can feel it in my bones," Hamish said. "Maybe somebody's hiding him—he could be working wi' an accomplice—but I know he's still here, and that means we can still catch the scunner."

Beyond Tommel Castle's impressive stone gateway, Hamish drove along an avenue of rhododendrons before crunching onto the gravel outside the main hotel building. Had Tommel Castle been a real clan fortress, it would doubtless have been left in ruins following some great siege centuries before. The fact that it was still standing, and that its battlements, turrets and spires bore no historic battle scars, betrayed its origins as a Victorian fantasy castle, built by a wealthy merchant in the nineteenth century when Queen Victoria and the new railways had made the Highlands the most fashionable place to own a country retreat.

Silas greeted them at the foot of the steps leading up to the main entrance. He was a good deal shorter than Hamish and, had the minimum height restrictions for police officers not been scrapped, he would never have made it through recruitment. As it turned out, policing was not his passion, even when working with Hamish, and he had been overjoyed when he was offered a job as the hotel's security manager.

"I've been patrolling the grounds at odd hours, Hamish," Silas informed him, "and the corridors as well. I've seen nothing out of the ordinary. None of the guests even remotely fits the description of your burglar."

"Aye, I doubted we would find him here," Hamish said.

"Keep on your toes, Silas, and if anyone here catches sight o' him, you let us know."

At that moment, the bridge team's crew bus drew into the car park and Stephanie Gibson jumped out. Silas nodded a greeting, then headed into the hotel, back to work.

"Well, well," she said, beaming a smile at Hamish. "Fancy meeting you here. Caught your burglar yet?"

"Umm…no," Hamish said, trying not to catch her eye. "The investigation is ongoing."

"I've just dropped the lads off at the pub," she said, "and I'm heading to the bar here for a drink myself. Are you two policemen still on duty or would you care to join me?"

"Actually, miss, that's a great idea," Bland said, rubbing his hands. "Come on, Hamish. It's been a long day. Let's relax a little."

"Aye," Hamish said. "It has been a long day. Maybe just the one, then."

"That's better!" Bland said, brightly. "Business and pleasure really do mix, you know!"

He offered Stephanie his arm and she linked in with him, Hamish reluctantly allowed her to loop her arm through his as well and the trio made their way up the hotel steps. Hamish would have turned tail and headed straight home to the sanctuary of his police station had he known what awaited him inside.

CHAPTER FIVE

When sorrows come, they come not single spies, but in battalions.

William Shakespeare, *Hamlet*

Stephanie, Hamish and Bland walked into the Tommel Castle's main bar, arms linked, Stephanie happily chatting and laughing about one of her lads who had slipped on the riverbank, ending up drenched. It took her a few moments to realize that Hamish had tensed and become even quieter than he had been outside. Then she saw Priscilla Halburton-Smythe standing in front of them.

Tall and elegant, with a glossy bell of blond hair, Priscilla was the colonel's daughter and had once been engaged to Hamish, much to her father's disapproval. He had expected his daughter to take up with a proper chap, a decent sort of some standing, not a lowly policeman. If the engagement was an embarrassment to him, however, the fact that Hamish had called it off had been little short of a disgrace. He, of course, was not to know that Hamish had found his daughter, although beautiful and desirable, to be a cold and dispassionate lover, ultimately concluding that she was not someone with whom he could spend the rest of his life.

"Good evening, Miss Gibson," Priscilla said, her lips parting in a smile that revealed perfectly aligned, delicately white teeth. "I see you've met our local police officers."

"Aye, I have," Stephanie replied, returning the smile, "and we're about to have a drink together."

Bland said hello to Priscilla, detached himself from the linked trio and made for the bar.

"I didn't realize you were here, Priscilla," Hamish said, slowly, always slightly wary of any encounter with his ex-fiancée. "I thought you were back in London again."

"I was, but I thought it would be nice to pay a visit before the winter weather sets in," Priscilla explained. "The truth is, I can do most of my job in London from here anyway, now that we have such good internet connections, and I enjoy helping out around here when I can."

"Aye, well I suppose it's a good idea to keep an eye on what's happening wi' your inheritance," Hamish said.

"That's one way of putting it," Priscilla said, frowning, "but I'm hoping my parents will be around for a long time yet."

"Och, aye, of course…" Hamish quickly replied. "I didn't mean you wanted to see them…I mean, you wouldn't want…"

"Stop digging, Hamish," Priscilla said, smiling and shaking her head. "You're already in a deep enough hole."

"That's not you putting your foot in it again, is it, Hamish?" Elspeth Grant walked into the bar, laughing. She was another to whom Hamish had once been engaged. Following her

dreams to work as a TV news reporter in Glasgow had ultimately led to them parting company, although Hamish was far
more comfortable around Elspeth than he was with Priscilla.
Elspeth had a gentle, affectionate nature and, while she had
developed a more glamorous image since leaving the Highlands, Hamish could still see the pretty young woman who
had once stolen his heart. Her captivating gray eyes were as
beguiling as ever, perhaps betraying the mystic "second sight"
psychic ability that had been passed down through genera-
tions of women in her family.

"Elspeth!" Hamish was even more surprised to see her
than he had been Priscilla. "I didn't know you were up from
Glasgow."

"Well, here I am anyway," Elspeth said, turning to Stephanie. "Aren't you going to introduce me to your new friend?"

Hamish stumbled through a basic introduction, Stephanie
still clinging doggedly to his arm.

"Another fiancée?" she said with a mischievous grin. "Are
there any attractive women in Lochdubh you haven't been
engaged to?"

"No, no, and…" Hamish hesitated. "This was all a long
time ago. So, what brings you home to Sutherland, Elspeth?"

"My boss got to hear about the wee matter of the army res-
cuing a stranded community by building them a bridge, so I've
been sent up to cover the story," Elspeth said. "I heard you had
a hand in all that."

"He did," Stephanie confirmed. "Rescued Mr. Patel and
his van from what everyone's calling the 'Anstey Bridge Disaster' and then called in the army."

"Great!" Elspeth said. "I'll need to interview you on camera when my team arrives and..."

"Och, you don't want to be doing that," Hamish said, shaking his head. "You know I'm not one for that kind of thing and, in any case, I'm supposed to have permission before talking to the press and...crivens!"

Hamish spotted a young woman walking across the reception area, heading into the bar. In an instant, he remembered that he was supposed to be somewhere else with someone else, and that someone else was now striding toward him with a look of undisguised fury on her face.

"Claire!" Hamish said, brushing Stephanie's hand free of his arm. "I'm so sorry—I completely forgot!"

"I can see that! You were supposed to meet me at the Napoli half an hour ago!" Claire snapped. She was wearing high heels and a shapely little black dress, a far cry from the baggy green paramedic uniform she'd been wearing when they had first met. "I thought I'd find you here when I saw your car going past, but I didn't think I'd find you with an entire... harem!"

Bland approached from the bar with a tray of drinks, took in what was happening at a glance, turned and made his way back to the bar. Priscilla, Elspeth and Stephanie mumbled excuses and hurried off to join him.

"I can explain," Hamish said desperately. "I've been rushing around all over the place and it's all been..."

"I know," Claire said, her angry look cooling to one of hopeless disappointment. "I've been busy, too, and the way my shifts work, evenings like this are precious to me."

"I'll make it up to you," Hamish offered. "I'll go home now and…"

"Don't bother, Hamish," she said, dismissing him with a wave of her hand and turning for the door. "I'm no' in the mood any more."

He watched her disappear out the front door, heard her high heels clicking down the stone steps, then felt a hand on his shoulder.

"Best let her cool down before you try talking to her again, buddy," Bland said, offering him a pint of beer. "Come on, have a drink and let us cheer you up a bit."

Hamish joined the small group at the bar but, try as they might, they couldn't brighten his dour mood. Priscilla and Elspeth advised him not to worry, assuring him he'd be able to win her round, while Stephanie added that, even if he couldn't, "There are plenty more fish in the sea." She grinned, giving a meaningful waggle of her eyebrows that made Elspeth laugh and Priscilla roll her eyes.

One drink became two, with two sliding into three, accompanied by some bar snacks in lieu of dinner before Hamish announced that they had a very early start in the morning and Bland agreed that they should get some rest. Having had three beers while Bland had drunk only his preferred Coke, Hamish handed him the car keys.

"I'll see you back there," he said. "I'll take a wee walk home to clear my heid."

He strolled down the driveway and turned to walk along the waterfront, where he was immediately aware of a group of young men larking around boisterously by the seawall, wrestling and attempting to topple each other over into the water.

"Be careful there, lads," he said, drawing closer and recognizing the group as Stephanie's bridge crew. "It doesn't look far to fall on the other side, but you can do yourself some damage on yon rocks below."

"Well, if it's no' the local bobby," said one, stepping forward to stand directly in front of Hamish. "Out lookin' for your burglar are you?"

"Steady on, Tam," said Kevin, the big digger driver. "We don't want any trouble."

Hamish looked at Kevin. He certainly wouldn't want to be involved in any kind of trouble. Falling foul of the law would mean breaching his parole and being recalled to prison. The others, however, were full of the swagger and bravado brought on by an evening in the pub.

"He'll never catch the burglar," a wiry young man called, laughing. "The burglar's out long after the official police bedtime!"

"It's your curfew time you need to be looking at, lads," Hamish said, tapping his watch. "If you're no' along at Mrs. Mackenzie's place by ten, she'll lock you out."

"Aye, last time that happened Tam had to climb in a window to let us in," said the wiry man. "Split his best breeks right up the back!"

"Well, I'm no' doin' that again!" Tam said, scowling at his friends. "So I'm away back there now."

"Good night, lads," Hamish said, watching them file past.

"Good luck wi' your burglar," said the wiry one, giving Hamish a wink.

Watching them sauntering along the street, jostling each other and laughing, Hamish decided that they probably weren't such a bad bunch. Put any group of half a dozen young men together, let them loose in the pub for a few hours and you'll get some lively behavior. Still, he thought, one of them had climbed in a window—a potential burglar? Yet none of them fitted the description. He shook his head as if to clear his thoughts and reminded himself that Mrs. Mackenzie's house was not as well maintained as it could be. He knew for a fact that the outside door locks would easily open with a little tinkering. The back door needed no more than a solid push. Any burglar worth his salt would have realized within a few minutes of being in the building that opening the locked back door would be preferable to ruining a pair of trousers.

"Split his best breeks," Hamish mumbled to himself, then laughed softly, walking off in the direction of the station.

The following morning, Hamish and Bland were up preparing for their trip south just as dawn's milky half-light was beginning to add some sparkle to the dark waters of Loch Dubh. Lugs and Sonsie, forever used to accompanying Hamish in the Land Rover, listened attentively as he told them they were to be left behind at home. Lugs looked heartbreakingly mournful while Sonsie appeared to be seething with a malevolent resentment, yet Hamish knew they would both be romping around down on the beach, chasing gulls, before he and Bland had crossed the bridge out of the village.

He was surprised to see Willie up and about when they drove past the Napoli, frantically cleaning the restaurant windows. Hamish pulled over to have a word.

"Early start today, Willie?" he said cheerfully.

"Aye, we've a coach party coming in," Willie explained.

"They took a detour on their way north to visit the Anstey Bridge Disaster! Lucia's in the kitchen already!"

"I doubt we'll eat as well as them today!" Hamish laughed, gunned the engine and set off for Strathbane.

When he and Bland walked into Superintendent Daviot's office just before eight, Daviot's loyal secretary, Helen, glowered at Hamish.

"Morning, Helen," Hamish said, giving her his biggest grin. "We'll be wanting coffee, I think, instead o' the usual tea, and maybe a wee bit o' toast instead o' biscuits, or possibly…"

"Superintendent Daviot has already dealt with that, Sergeant," she hissed.

"Is that you, Macbeth?" Daviot called from his inner office. "Get in here and let's get on with this. I have a busy day ahead."

"Keep smiling, Helen!" Hamish gave her a wink before strolling in to meet her boss.

To his amazement, Daviot had a pot of coffee on his desk and three plates loaded with bacon sandwiches.

"I was up a little too early for Mrs. Daviot to prepare breakfast this morning," he said, "so I picked up these on the way in. Do help yourselves, gentlemen. Now, what can I tell you about these damn spies?"

"You were the senior investigating officer in a case involving a Strathbane Savings Bank employee, Tommy Carter, who went missing along with over two hundred thousand pounds," Bland said.

"That is correct," Daviot confirmed, "and, as you already know, DCIs Anderson and Blair were both sergeants on my team at that time."

"We also know that the bank manager, Morgan Mackay, staged the disappearance to make it look like Carter had run off with the cash," Bland went on, "because Carter had found out that Mackay was responsible for some dubious transactions at the bank."

"Also correct," said Daviot, "as Sergeant Macbeth found out when he took Mackay's deathbed confession."

"Mackay said your name was on a list," Hamish said, passing a sheet of paper bearing the names of the Dozen across the desk, "along with these folk. They all received payouts from him as the spy-ring paymaster, but you were listed only because he thought you were getting close and he was considering trying to buy you off."

"I would stress that, to the best of my knowledge, none of us was ever offered and never accepted any sort of payment from Mackay," Daviot said, sitting rigidly upright as though to stress that he was as straight as his back.

"Do any of the other names mean anything to you, sir?" Bland asked. "We're interested in William McAllister, James Smith and John Martin."

"Nothing at all," Daviot said, shaking his head. "Since you first showed me the list, I've been through old case files and notes and I can say with some confidence that I have never come across any of these men."

Hamish munched on his bacon sandwich, watching Daviot examining Bland's photographs and answering a few more questions. He could tell Daviot was being totally honest with them. The superintendent was, basically, an honest man and would never have allowed himself to become involved with anything underhand. Jimmy Anderson, he knew, didn't always set his standards quite so high but was also a good, decent police officer. Blair, on the other hand, was a different breed altogether. With his bacon sandwich finished, he took a last gulp of coffee, stood and clapped some crumbs off his hands.

"Well, I think we'd best have a wee word with DCI Anderson now," he said, Bland following him to the outer office.

"Did you no' get a bacon sandwich, Helen?" he asked, raising his eyebrows when she looked up from her computer screen. "Mr. Daviot has a wee bit left if you fancy it."

"I do not..." she started to attempt a rebuke but Hamish was already out in the corridor. Bland gave her a wave and a smile before closing the door.

DCI Jimmy Anderson flicked through Bland's photographs, laughed at the one showing Blair in uniform at the peace camp, and handed them back. Hamish studied his old friend. Jimmy's foxy face and sharp eyes were looking keen and intense. He was looking healthier and more alert than he had done in years, testament to the fact that, following a car crash where he had been over the drink-drive limit, and a spell in hospital that had helped him to dry out, Jimmy had his drinking under control.

"The Tommy Carter case was a strange affair," Jimmy said after a long round of questions. "We never found the poor laddie or any o' the money. All our leads were dead ends. Then the cloak-and-dagger mob showed up and shut us down, threatening us wi' the Official Secrets Act and all sorts. We never knew anything about any spies until Hamish rattled their cage a while back."

"Do you think DCI Blair will be any more help?" Bland asked.

"Ha! I doubt it!" Jimmy laughed. "I mind when the men from MI5 arrived in the office. Nobody knew who they were. Then we were both summoned to Daviot's office and Blair just about filled his breeks! He thought he was in big trouble. God knows what he'd been up to, but it wouldn't have had anything to do wi' espionage. He hasn't got the brains for that."

"We're off down to Glasgow to talk to him next," Hamish said.

"Well, you be careful down there, laddie," Jimmy said waving a warning finger at Hamish. "Blair has a lot o' contacts wi' the Macgregor family in Glasgow and the last time you tangled wi' that bunch o' cutthroats, you jailed their boss but you near ended up dead."

"Don't worry, sir," Bland said, brightly. "I'll look after him."

"Aye, right," Jimmy said, nodding gravely. "See you do."

The route Hamish and Bland took to Glasgow saw them cross Sutherland to Inverness where they drove south on the A9, skirting the Cairngorm mountain range before dropping down into Perthshire and heading southwest to Glasgow. The whole journey took four hours with just one stop for coffee, fuel and to change drivers. Hamish was glad that Bland was at the wheel when they hit the Glasgow traffic. Once known as "The Second City of the British Empire" and still Scotland's largest center of population with almost two million inhabitants in its whole, sprawling conurbation, Glasgow made Hamish feel distinctly uncomfortable. The noise, the traffic, the mass of buildings and the energy of the place were, for some, what made Glasgow such an exciting city. For Hamish, they all combined to make him feel small, claustrophobic and desperate to return to his home in Lochdubh.

His phone rang as they drove toward the city center. It was Blair.

"Are you no' here yet?" he bawled down the phone.

"Obviously, if we're no' wi' you and you're phoning me, then we're no' there yet," Hamish replied.

"Don't you get lippy wi' me, Macbeth! Afore we sit down, I want to make it crystal clear that I am a detective chief inspector and I demand to be interviewed by someone of equal or superior rank."

"Well, that's no' going to happen," Hamish said, rubbing his brow. "You're no' under caution or under arrest, you're just helping us figure out who we're looking for."

"In that case," Blair growled, "I'll no' be talking to you on police premises. You can meet me in a pub, and don't come in uniform."

He gave them the address of a pub he referred to as "the Hairy Arms" then hung up.

"I have a couple of sweaters in the back of the car," Hamish said. "We'd best do as he asks or he'll no' talk to us at all, despite whatever letter you might wave in his face."

"Why won't he meet us in his office?" Bland asked.

"Because he's a head case," Hamish said, tucking his phone into his pocket. "He won't want anyone seeing him being 'interviewed' by us because it would be an embarrassment—a loss o' face. Also, he'll take any chance he can get to have a drink."

"The interviews with Daviot and Anderson were a bit dull,"

Bland said, laughing, "but this sounds like it could be a lot more fun!"

They found a car park where they could leave the police Land Rover and pulled on woolen sweaters. One was gray with a blue Fair Isle pattern around the yoke, the other was forest green with leather patches on the shoulders and elbows. Wearing the green sweater seemed to make Hamish's shock of red hair even more conspicuously ginger and, at well over six feet tall, he would certainly stand out in a crowd, but at least they were no longer recognizably in uniform.

The pub Blair had chosen for their meeting was in one of the dingiest areas of the city, and they walked along a street of red sandstone tenement buildings where the twin magic wands of modernization and gentrification had yet to cast their spell. Turning right at the street corner, they found the pub on the opposite side of the road. The painted pub sign suspended above the door showed a flexed, very muscular and extremely hairy arm. The pub windows were opaque, frosted glass, a throwback to the days when it was considered undesirable for children to be corrupted or decent people to be affronted by the sight of uncouth drinkers carousing inside.

Hamish scanned the pub as they walked in. A few men were drinking at the far end of the bar, which looked remarkably clean and polished compared with the rest of the room. A few more sat at a scattering of cheap wooden chairs and tables in front of the bar and a series of booths along one wall. There were no women in the pub. He saw Blair sitting in one of the booths, wearing a nondescript gray anorak. When Hamish caught his eye, Blair's jowly features shook, and his eyes widened with alarm. He beckoned them over.

"What the hell are you buggers dressed like?" he growled, staring at Hamish. "Look at you, wi' your green jumper and red hair. You look like an overgrown elf! And him wi' his fancy knit—nobody looks like that around here!"

"It was this or uniform," Hamish said, motioning Bland to take a seat in the booth.

"For God's sake, get me a drink," Blair said, draining his whisky glass, "and make it a double! Let's get this ower wi' as quick as possible."

Hamish stepped up to the bar, ordered their drinks and saw, out of the corner of his eye, a few of the regulars staring at him, then muttering to each other. What was the matter with them? Had they never seen an overgrown elf before? He ignored them, paid for the drinks and took them back to the booth. Blair was horrified.

"What in the name o' the wee man are you two drinking?" he said, wincing. "Coke? Soda water? You couldn't do any more to draw attention to yourselves aside from turnin' up in a police motor wi' the blue lights on."

"We did," Hamish informed him. "No' wi' the lights on, but we left my Land Rover in a car park a couple o' streets away."

Blair tutted and wiped his hand down his face, glancing anxiously around the bar to gauge the reaction of the other drinkers.

"Hurry up," he said. "I don't want to be seen wi' you. What do you want to know?"

Hamish and Bland posed the same questions they had put to Daviot and Jimmy, receiving one-word replies. Blair knew nothing about the spy ring. Photographs were passed surreptitiously under the table.

"You policed the peace camp at Faslane while you were still in uniform," Bland said, having shown Blair the photo.

"Aye, there was a few o' us sent up there once in a while," Blair replied.

"Did you know the woman in that photo—Alex Black?" Hamish asked.

"I mind o' seein' her a few times." Blair nodded, shuffling a little in his seat in a manner that Hamish took to be a show of either nervousness or troublesome hemorrhoids. "She was a good-lookin' lassie. She was ay searched and she was ay caught wi' the marijuana."

"You searched her?" asked Bland.

"Don't be daft, Yank," Blair sneered at him. "A female officer searched her. She was the type that would have screamed the place down and had the press all over us if any o' the lads had gone near her."

Hamish pressed him a little harder, but Blair denied any further knowledge of Alex Black or any of the protesters, so he decided to change tack.

"Have you heard anything about a recent suicide—a man called Edward Chalmers?" Hamish asked.

"Aye, I've heard a few tales," Blair said, downing his whisky. "I wasn't involved in the investigation, but folk are saying that it definitely wasn't a suicide. The word is that someone from out of town, somewhere up north, paid two local hard men to kill Chalmers and make it look like an accident or suicide. They went right ower the top wi' the fire—attracted too much attention—but there was no evidence for anythin' other than suicide. That's the official verdict."

"Chalmers was one of the Dozen," Bland said. "Are there any rumors about why he was killed?"

"Nothin' about spies—folk are guessin' drugs, gamblin' debts, the usual sort o' thing," Blair answered, taking a swig of whisky.

"And what about this person up north who ordered Chalmers's death?" Hamish asked. "Is he a Scot or a foreigner?"

"A Russian, you mean?" said Blair. "No, I told you. Nobody's talkin' about spies and…Och, no…" He cringed and buried his face in his hands.

A thickset man with a shaved head, wearing a black leather jacket and jeans, walked up to their booth.

"Hey, you!" he said, prodding Hamish's shoulder. "You're yon Hamish Macbeth, are you no'?"

"Who wants to know?" Hamish asked, tensing.

"Aye, we thought as much," the man said, suddenly swinging a punch at Hamish's head. Hamish jerked his head backward, dodging the flying fist, and slapped the man's wrist, sending the punch into the table. He then pushed himself to his feet, driving his own fist into the man's stomach. By the time Hamish was upright, his assailant had recovered and was making to throw another punch when the heel of Hamish's right hand slammed into his chest. He staggered backward, crashing into a table, sending drinks flying, smashing glasses and scattering those who had been seated there.

Having their beer knocked into their laps brought howls of outrage from the disturbed drinkers, who rounded on the shaven-headed man. Friends joined in on either side with a short round of pushing, shoving, shouting and swearing swiftly developing into a wrestling match with punches thrown and, in the blink of an eye, the bar was embroiled in a full-scale brawl.

"You okay?" Bland asked, standing shoulder-to-shoulder with Hamish and viewing the brawl with disbelief. "That's like the Wild West."

"Aye, and it's coming our way," Hamish said, the thunder of feet on the uncarpeted floor and the roars and grunts of the combatants growing even louder as the melee engulfed them.

"Make for the door, James!" Hamish yelled, fending off one attacker and throwing another aside. A wooden chair sailed through the air and glanced off the side of his head. He stumbled sideways and then found himself out on the street, the quiet rumble of passing traffic a stark contrast to the cacophony in the pub. His fingers explored the graze left by the airborne chair.

"We need to get out of here, James," he said. "Otherwise we'll be caught up in it all when the police arrive and…" He realized he was talking to himself. Bland was not there.

He rushed back into the bar in time to see a stream of men making quickly for what was clearly a rear exit. The brawl had subsided as quickly as it had begun and only a couple of older regulars remained, calmly sipping beer in the booth from which they had never moved. With no sign of Bland inside, he followed the others out into a side street but could still find no trace of his friend.

Dashing back into the bar, he found the barman contemplating the shambles that he now had to clear up.

"Have you seen my friend?" Hamish asked. "The one wi' the fancy jumper."

"No, I've no' seen anybody," the barman answered flatly. "They've all legged it, and you'd better do the same afore the cops get here."

Hamish looked over to the booth where they had been sitting, realizing that he hadn't seen Blair since the fracas began. No doubt he had made an early exit. He noticed Bland's document folder lying on the seat where he had left it and grabbed it before leaving. Back out in the street, he reasoned that Bland would have gone back to their car and began walking in that direction, plucking his phone from his pocket. He got no answer from Bland's phone and, when he called Blair's office, he was told that the DCI was "out on inquiries." Hearing the siren of an approaching police car, he quickened his pace toward the car park.

When he reached his Land Rover, however, there was still no sign of Bland. He climbed in and cruised the area, street by street, but still couldn't find him and still couldn't raise him on the phone.

"James," he whispered to himself. "Where are you? What's going on? What's happened to you?"

Then he thought of Blair again. If something had happened to James, Blair was sure to know about it. He knew everything that happened on his patch, and anything he didn't know, he could find out. There was one person Hamish could be sure would know where Blair was—his wife, Mary. Hamish had introduced Mary, a former sex worker with a heart of gold, to Blair years before. She knew how best to deal with her idiot husband, and how best to maintain the marriage that afforded her a comfortable lifestyle. Hamish called her.

"Mary, it's Hamish," he said as soon as she answered. "Don't say anything. I need to know if he's there wi' you."

"Aye, that's such a shame, Denise," Mary replied. "Well, you can't run a salon wi' no hot water, can you?"

"Okay, Mary, I take it he's there and he can hear you," Hamish said. "I need to come round and see him. Keep him there, will you?"

"Aye, plumbers are right hard to find, are they no'?" Mary said. "He's there now? He'll be there all night? Well, that should get the job done."

"Thanks, Mary," Hamish said. "I'm coming now."

He headed north of the River Clyde and west to Hyndland, an area of Glasgow he had seldom visited, although he knew precisely where the Blairs lived. They had an opulent apartment in a four-story, sandstone tenement block that was a far cry from the seedy area surrounding the Hairy Arms. In Hyndland there were tree-lined avenues, gourmet cafés, expensive delicatessens and chic coffee shops where middle-class mothers met after dropping their children at school. It was an area where Blair could easily afford to live on his salary as a DCI, but would never have chosen. Their apartment was Mary's dream home and Hamish knew that she controlled the purse strings in their relationship, preventing Blair from squandering his pay on booze and horses. Blair had his wife to thank for his little sanctuary in Hyndland.

Hamish shook his head at the thought of the brawl in the Hairy Arms. That was like something from Glasgow's distant, brutal past. The city was now a sophisticated, cosmopolitan center of commerce and culture, having shed its reputation for violence along with so much of its heavy industry. Hyndland was part of modern Glasgow, and was seen as a desirable area to live, yet, as far as Hamish was concerned, the Glaswegians could keep it all to themselves. All he wanted to do was to get back north to Lochdubh, and to do that, he had to find Bland.

He parked out of sight of the large bay windows at the front of the Blairs' top-floor apartment, let himself in through the security door using a code that hadn't changed since his last visit, and bounded up the stairs three at a time. Mary opened the door when he knocked and he could see past her to where Blair stood, frozen with disbelief, across the hall in the living-room doorway, a glass of whisky in his hand.

"What?" he mumbled as Hamish strode toward him. "What are you doin' here?"

"Where is he?" demanded Hamish.

"Where's who?" Blair replied. "What are you talking about?"

"James—Sergeant Bland—he went missing along wi' that crowd in yon stinkin' pub o' yours! He's no' answering his phone!"

"Oh, shite..." Blair groaned, turning into the living room and lowering himself into an armchair.

"Who were those eejits?" Hamish shouted, towering over the cowering Blair. "Why did one o' them pick a fight wi' me? Have they got James?"

"Who do you think they were?" Blair said, staring up at Hamish with a look of pity that Hamish couldn't see what was, to him, so obvious. "Who down here would want to have a go at you? They were part o' the Macgregor gang, Macbeth. You put their boss behind bars and everyone that works for them knows it. Even if they've never seen you, they all know what you look like. You're a marked man down here in the city. Every wee shite that wants to make his name as a hard man would love to be able to say he gave Hamish Macbeth a smack in the teeth.

"So when you walked in the pub—all six-foot-umpteen o' you—wi' the ginger hair and the Highland teuchter accent, they took notice. Aye, 'overgrown elf' I said, standin' out like a sore thumb, and I was right, was I no'? Then, when they saw you talking to me, they knew exactly who you were. That's why they picked a fight wi' you."

"Aye, and you were pretty slick at ducking out o' that, weren't you?" Hamish snarled. "So what about James? Have they got him?"

"More than likely," Blair said, quietly. "They'll have taken him to get to you. You'll no doubt get a call once they've worked out what to do. Maybe they'll use him as bait to lure you into a trap, but they'll need to go up their chain o' command. The big boss might no' want the heat that kidnappin' a Yank cop working wi' British police will bring. Whoever took him will play it canny until they get instructions."

"Where would they take him?" Hamish asked, then bridled at Blair's reluctance to reply. "Come on, Blair! You know these folk! Where would they take him?"

"Somewhere close by," Blair said, nodding, thinking hard. "They have a warehouse a few streets away from the pub. Maybe there."

"Take me there, now!" Hamish snapped.

"You must be right off your heid!" Blair responded. "It's dangerous enough for me that I was seen in the pub wi' you. I'm definitely no' going anywhere near yon warehouse!"

"I'll take you," Mary said, suddenly. "I used to work the

streets around there. I know the warehouse. We can go in my car."

"Fine," Hamish said, giving Blair a look of utter contempt. "Let's go."

Mary knew a few shortcuts taking them back toward the Hairy Arms and parked her small hatchback in a side street.

"That's the warehouse over there," she said pointing toward a shabby light-industrial unit.

"Thanks, Mary," Hamish said, patting her hand. "I couldn't have come this close in the police Land Rover without being spotted. You can leave me here."

"Leave you?" Mary laughed. "Don't be such a dunderheid. If your pal's in there, and you can get him out, you need somebody waitin' out here. A getaway driver."

"Getaway driver?" Hamish said, raising an eyebrow. "This isn't some kind o' game, Mary. You should go."

"Well, I'm no' goin' anywhere," Mary said, stubbornly, folding her arms.

"Aye, right," Hamish said, then paused on seeing two men coming out of the warehouse front door. "That one wi' the shaved head started the fight in the pub. Maybe your auld man was right. James must be in there."

The two men got into a car and drove off. There were a few other parked cars in the street but no passing traffic and no pedestrians in sight.

"If you're goin' to take a look, you can try down that alley." Mary pointed to the side of the warehouse. "There's a back door down there."

"All right," Hamish said, taking a deep breath. "Stay out of sight, Mary, and keep your phone handy."

Mary watched him lever his lanky frame out of the small car and walk briskly across the road toward the warehouse.

"Take care, Hamish Macbeth," she said softly to herself, seeing him disappear down the alleyway, "you great overgrown elf…"

CHAPTER SIX

Every man is surrounded by a neighborhood of voluntary spies.

Jane Austen, *Northanger Abbey*

Inside the warehouse, in a grimy office lit by the yellowish light from a low-watt bulb, two men stood talking nervously. Both wore jeans, one with a black hoodie and the other with a black bomber jacket. Neither looked happy to be there and both glanced down from time to time at a third man, gagged and bound to a wooden chair. Their prisoner, James Bland, met their looks with a defiant glare.

"I hope they're no' goin' to be long," said the man in the hoodie. He had a thin, anxious face and was a good deal younger than his friend in the bomber jacket.

"Aye, I hope no'," his friend concurred. "I don't want to be stuck in this dump all night."

"They're bound to come up wi' something soon, are they no'?" said the first man. "I mean, they can't keep him here forever, can they?"

"No, it's too risky. They'll decide if he's any use to them," said the older man, turning to their prisoner, "and you'd better hope you are, pal, otherwise you'll end up at the bottom o' the Clyde."

Hamish picked his way down the alley at the side of the warehouse as stealthily as he could. Although it was only late afternoon, the narrow space was gloomy, daylight struggling to penetrate between its high walls, and the pathway was scattered with discarded bottles and cans, as well as windblown litter. The place reeked of decay and stale urine, clearly having been used in extremis by late-night revelers caught short on their way home.

He found the warehouse back door toward the end of the alley. It was locked. He took a small wallet from his pocket, a lockpick set given to him many years before by a wily old safe breaker. It took only a few seconds to spring the lock and he dodged inside, gently pushing the door closed behind him. He was now in almost total darkness and waited a few moments for his eyes to become used to the lack of light.

Once he was able to make out that he was in a storeroom, the walls of which were lined with shelves stacked with boxes, he crept toward a door that he assumed led into the main warehouse. Opening the door just a crack, he could see a dimly lit space illuminated only by the light seeping through a few grimy glass panels in the roof. Crates and boxes were piled around the periphery, close to the walls, along with various items of construction equipment and what looked like an old car under a tarpaulin.

The only part of the premises that was properly lit was a

corner that had been sectioned off with wooden paneling set with windows, clearly some kind of office. From where he was, he couldn't see into the office. He needed to get closer. Easing the door open a little further, he slipped through the gap into the shadows. The clutter of crates provided good cover for him to be able to creep toward the office, staying low and hugging the darkness, moving silently and pausing every few seconds to check for any untoward sounds or signs of anyone else sneaking around the premises.

Just a few meters from the office, he reached a stack of boxes tall enough for him to be able to stand while still remaining out of sight. From his hiding place, he could see straight in through one of the office windows. Two men stood talking, although he couldn't hear what they were saying. Another man was seated. It was James, his wrists and ankles bound to the arms and legs of his chair with gaffer tape that had also been used to gag him. Hamish felt a sudden urge to rush into the office yelling "Police" and arrest the two thugs, but he forced himself to stay put. He had no backup. There was no one there to help him. He might be able to subdue one of the two men long enough to cuff him, but James was helpless should the other man turn on him. He needed to think this through. Slowly, he crouched in the darkness.

Before he did anything, he had to work out exactly what he was dealing with. He could see no sign that either of the men holding James was armed. Maybe they weren't senior enough in the Macgregor organization to be trusted with firearms, or maybe they were smart enough to know that they'd be facing a long time in a prison cell if they were caught with an illegal gun. Unlike James's home in the United States, guns were not commonplace in Britain, even among the criminal fraternity.

So, no guns. That was good. Now, were there really only two of them? Hamish scanned the rest of the warehouse and crept around the walls, moving silently behind the boxes, making sure he stayed out of sight. His reconnaissance took several minutes, but he found no sign of anyone else. Clearly, the two in the office had been left to guard the prisoner until it could be decided what to do with him. They didn't look like prizefighters, yet he couldn't rely on being able to handle both of them. What he needed was for one of them to disappear for a few moments. Maybe Mary could help. Of course! He scolded himself. He wasn't entirely without backup. He had Mary outside.

Crouching in the darkness again, he fished his phone out of his pocket. Shielding it between some boxes so that its screen didn't light up his hiding place when he switched it on, he checked that it was in silent mode and sent a text message to Mary: "Need a loud diversion outside in 2 mins." She was a smart lassie. She'd think of something. He made his way back to his position close to the office and waited.

Two minutes later the sound of a car alarm filled the warehouse, followed by another, then another, each one different and each apparently louder and more strident than the one before. The cacophony seemed to be amplified in the open space inside the building, making it sound even more urgent. From where he was hiding, Hamish saw the two men burst out of the office door.

"Bloody hell!" the younger man cursed. "What's going on out there? Is that your car?"

"It better no' be!" spat the older man. "Anybody messes wi' my motor's a dead man! Bide here! I'll see what's happenin'!"

He strode off toward the front door, wrenched it open and let it slam behind him. The younger man was still staring after his friend when Hamish hit him from behind, knocking the wind out of him and wrestling him to the ground. With practiced ease, he pinned his adversary's chest to the floor with a knee in his back, yanked his arms behind him and snapped handcuffs on his wrists. He then dragged the man into the office and, grabbing the roll of gaffer tape that had been used to bind Bland, taped his ankles. Even if he'd had the breath to shout and yell, his friend outside would not have heard above the din of the car alarms. Hamish slapped a strip of tape across his mouth anyway.

Using a penknife from his pocket, it took only moments to cut the tape at Bland's wrists and ankles. Bland ripped the tape off his own mouth.

"Are you all right, James?" Hamish asked.

"I'm just peachy," Bland said through gritted teeth.

"Come on, this way!" Hamish said, heading for the back door.

"Be right with you," Bland replied, kneeling on the floor beside the squirming man. He took a fistful of hoodie, dragging the man's face toward his. "You can tell your buddy outside," he snarled with quiet menace, "that next time I'm back in town it will be to come find you two assholes!" He patted the man gently on the cheek and let him drop back to the floor.

They sneaked up the alley, Hamish signaling for Bland to stop near its entrance. He took a quick look out into the street and saw the man in the black bomber jacket standing on the pavement about two hundred meters away, remonstrating with two others. A couple of the cars had broken side widows. Bland's former captor had his back to them. Walking confidently and casually, trying not to attract attention, Hamish and Bland crossed the street to where Mary was waiting in the side road. Her car was parked just where she had been before but facing in the opposite direction, ready to go. They both climbed in and she pulled away, heading for Hyndland.

"You two really like to live dangerously," she said, shaking her head. "Why did you no' just call in your police pals to deal wi' this? You're just ordinary blokes, you know, no' superheroes. I had to take one hell o' a risk settin' off yon alarms."

"Aye and thanks for that, Mary," Hamish said, "but we've no' got time to get stuck here in Glasgow answering questions all night for the local boys." He neglected to add that they had no idea whom they could trust on the local force. Anyone in the pay of the Macgregors would have let the gang know they were coming to spring James and he would immediately have been moved from the warehouse, perhaps never to be seen again.

"And I'd be in big trouble with my bosses if word got back to them that I'd gotten involved in a bar brawl," Bland added, grinning. "So you saved my skin in more ways than one, Mary."

Hamish, sitting in the front passenger seat, turned to look at Bland. He doubted his friend would have had any problems with his superiors, but he knew that he and Mary had rescued him from something far worse. He could now count at least part of his debt to the American as repaid.

"Did you get hurt?" he asked.

"I'm okay," Bland replied, rubbing his wrist where the tape had dug in. "Just a bit embarrassed about being bushwhacked like that—and real grateful to both of you."

"You need to get out o' the city," Mary advised, "quick as you can. Right now all flavors o' shit will be hittin' the Macgregor fan."

Hamish and Bland took Mary's advice, transferring to the Land Rover as soon as they were back in Hyndland and joining the early evening traffic on the motorway heading east out of Glasgow.

"You know," Bland said from the passenger seat, Hamish having volunteered to drive the first leg of the route home, "before all that business with the pub fight, I got the distinct impression that Blair was keeping something from us. He knew Alex Black all right, and admitted it, but there was more he wasn't saying."

"Aye, I was thinking the same," Hamish agreed, nodding. "Blair's slippery as a greased weasel but there's one thing you can ay count on wi' him. If he sounds like he's lying, and he looks like he's lying, then whatever he's saying is definitely no' the truth."

"Do you think he could be involved with the Dozen?" Bland asked. "Is he one of those names we can't trace?"

"I'd say no." Hamish was quite positive. "He was elsewhere on the list, along wi' Daviot and Jimmy, remember. Besides, it's just no' his style. He's ay done a bit o' ducking and diving as a cop, swapping favors for information and doubtless taking the odd cash backhander now and again, but he'd be feared to get mixed up wi' spies and suchlike. He was born and raised among hard men and criminals but the espionage stuff is way out o' his league. It's no' part o' his world and he'd be terrified o' getting sucked into all that."

"Yet you still think he was lying when we talked to him about Alex Black."

"Aye, I've no doubt he was, but we'll get nothing more out of him. I think we now need to talk to Alex Black—or Moira Stephenson as I know her."

Hamish's phone rang and he answered it using the car's hands-free system, Lachlan's voice suddenly filling the Land Rover.

"Hamish, how are you doing?" said the old policeman. "How did you get on looking at yon crash site at Applecross? You didn't come by to let me know."

"Aye, well we've been awfy busy, Lachlan," Hamish said, "out and about a lot, you know?"

"Did it help you wi' your missing-person case?" Lachlan asked.

"We're no' really sure," Hamish said, playing his cards close to his chest. "No doubt we'll find out more in due course."

"And what about my missing person—Jean Graham?" Lachlan asked. "Anything you can help me wi' there?"

"You don't need to worry about her, Lachlan," Hamish assured him. "She's no' missing. We saw her near Applecross and spoke wi' her. She's taken herself off into the hills, that's all. Nothing sinister there."

"I see…" Lachlan said, slowly, as though he were thinking. "I thought it might have something to do with her friend, Carol McGill, and her father up in Thurso. You see, I hear the

McGills have gone missing as well. Anything you can tell me about that? Any idea where they might be?"

"Well, that's no' really my patch, Lachlan," Hamish said, frowning at Bland. "I've no idea where they might have gone."

"And just who is your missing person?" Lachlan asked.

"Och, nobody you need worry about," Hamish said, sounding as if he meant to set Lachlan's mind at ease but with a curious look on his face. "I think that will all turn out to be a waste o' time, as these things sometimes do, a bit like your Jean Graham."

"Well, let me know if you hear anything about the McGills, Hamish," Lachlan said. "It's just…well, call it professional interest."

They said a slightly awkward goodbye and Bland, having remained silent throughout the exchange, looked across at Hamish.

"What was that all about?" he asked. "You sounded like you were being real cautious with your old buddy."

"Aye, well…" Hamish was running the conversation through his head. "That was just a wee bit strange. I've known Lachlan for years and we speak every once in a while. I've never known him to take any interest whatsoever in anything happening outside his patch around Lochcarron."

"Cops like to talk about cases," Bland said. "It's how they reassure themselves that they're all in the same boat—all dealing with the same old stuff."

"True," Hamish agreed, "but Lachlan's never quizzed me like that afore. He works hard but he's ay been one to give you the impression that he's just cruising toward retirement— putting in the years afore putting his feet up. Something must be bothering him. I'll have a wee word wi' him when we've got more time."

The traffic eased once they were on the road to Stirling and bottlenecked at roadworks around Perth but they made good progress back up the A9 toward Inverness. Hamish took a slight detour near Newtonmore where they stopped at the Newtonmore Grill for a meal of burgers with all the trimmings followed by apple crumble. If Bland had been affected in any way by the trauma of being kidnapped, it had made no impact on his appetite, and he cleared his plate.

"So," he said, sipping a coffee, "I don't think we're now in any doubt that Chalmers and Graham were murdered."

"Aye, it certainly looks that way," Hamish agreed, "and McGill has gone into hiding, as has his daughter and Jean Graham. They're all feared for their lives—but why? Why the murders?"

"My guess would be that the Russians want the network up and running again," Bland said. "What they won't want is any of the old-timers messing it up. If they're not one hundred percent on side any more, they might be tempted to talk to the British secret service. Anyone who might know too much about the Ruskies' organization but who has any doubts about continuing to play ball becomes a liability—a risk to any future operations. They're eliminating the risks."

"Aye, I've seen how they deal wi' folk they're no' friends wi' any longer," said Hamish, polishing off the last of his apple crumble, "but I'm no' so interested in all yon spy stuff. What bothers me is that we've got a murderer, or murderers, running around the country—that's getting right up my nose."

"And we're no further forward in finding out who they are," Bland pointed out.

"Aye, but we are," Hamish argued. "You can't always rely on rumors, but when folk are spreading tales, they like to make the story as juicy as possible. If it had been a Russian who ordered Chalmers's murder, or anybody wi' a foreign accent, that would be part o' the story. Blair was adamant that whoever ordered Chalmers's death was not a Russian, and I believed him on that."

"You reckon whoever's behind the killings is a Scot? Maybe one of the Dozen?"

"Aye, but mind—your twelve are now only six. Four died o' natural causes ower the years and two have been recently murdered. O' the remaining six, I've met Moira Stephenson and I can tell you that she's no killer. McGill is in hiding, so he's more likely to be a potential victim than a murderer."

"That leaves four," Bland nodded. "McAllister, Smith and Martin we know nothing about. Robb we know is up in Durness."

"And there were four involved in the Graham murder," Hamish pointed out. "We need to talk to Robb. In fact, tomorrow we need to take a big tour. We'll find out a bit more about McGill and try to track him down. He'll be able to tell us about the three mystery men. We'll talk to Robb and see what we can get out o' him, and it's high time we had a word wi' Moira Stephenson."

"What about our burglar in Lochdubh?"

"There's something a wee bit strange going on there," Hamish said, running his hand through his hair and pondering the problem for the thousandth time. "There's something I'm missing—something I'm just no' seeing." He sighed. "I'll work it out soon enough."

It was almost midnight by the time Bland parked the Land Rover in its space outside the police station in Lochdubh. Lugs and Sonsie offered their usual welcome, each in his or her own style, before Bland headed for his bedroom and Hamish took a quick shower before falling into bed. It was a warm night and he lay for a while in the darkness, banning all thoughts of spies and murderers from his mind to try to visualize the tattooed burglar. Inevitably, however, his mind drifted back to the pub fight and the warehouse before he finally drifted off to sleep.

Two hours later, in their apartment above the Napoli, Lucia was having a tougher time trying to sleep. She'd had a busy day in the kitchen feeding the coachload of tourists who had booked in, as well as an unexpectedly hectic sitting of evening bookings. She'd had help from a trusted local lad in the kitchen and Willie had had a waitress working with him out in the restaurant, but having the extra staff had made it all seem even more frenetic. She still had scores of food orders replaying in her head over and over again. Slipping out of bed, leaving Willie sleeping soundly, she pulled on a robe and made her way downstairs to the kitchen where moonlight was streaming in through the back window. Willie had, as he always did, cleaned and cleared everything away immaculately.

Leaving the lights off, she unlocked the back door that led to the small area of decking looking out over the loch. Having done the same so many times before, she knew that if she just sat there for a few minutes, watching the moonlight shimmering on the water, she would be able to absorb its calming influence and sleep would come more easily when she went back to bed. She opened the door and looked up at the moon.

Suddenly a gloved hand was clamped over her mouth and an arm wrapped round her waist, pinning her arms to her sides. Eyes wide with terror, scarcely able to breathe, she was half-dragged, half-carried backward into the kitchen, her feet barely touching the floor. She was slammed into a work surface and her arms were released, only for her to feel one of her own kitchen knives at her throat.

"Make a sound and I'll slit your bonny throat!" a man's voice hissed and she found herself looking into the bluest eyes she had ever seen. "Now—where's the cash?"

Lucia was trembling, stunned, shocked and horrified. Her legs felt as if they had no strength and she knew that if it weren't for the rough hand gripping her face and her attacker's body pressed against hers, she would have sunk to the floor. Slowly, she raised a shaking hand to point toward the office, just off the kitchen.

"In there, then," came the whispered command. "Not a sound, mind, or I swear I'll cut you!"

They moved together in a hideous, shuffling dance into the office, the man stepping behind her but the knife never leaving her throat. Like the kitchen, the office was lit only by the moon and she crossed to a desk on which stood a computer screen and keyboard.

"The money—get it!" he instructed. "No sudden moves—no noise."

He bent with Lucia, the steel blade threatening to break the skin on her neck, as she unlocked a desk drawer, reaching in to retrieve a red cash box with a combination lock.

"Open it!"

Lucia had a moment of dread when she thought she might not remember the combination, but it came to her as soon as her fingers touched the dials. She opened the lid of the cash box to reveal a neat stack of notes. Most of their customers that day had paid by card, but there was still several hundred pounds in the box, waiting to be banked. The man grabbed the notes and she could hear him stuffing them into a pocket.

"Now—back to the kitchen," he grunted.

He shoved her back against the work surface and reached for an apron, dangling the strings to judge their length.

"This will do to tie you," he judged, and for a moment, he let the knife drop from her neck. Alert to his distraction, Lucia summoned all her courage, closing her fingers around the handle of a heavy saucepan and smashing it into the side of his face with a mighty howl of fear-stoked rage.

"Willie!" she screamed. "Willie!"

The man staggered, stunned by the blow, holding his face. A drip of blood from a small cut on his cheek stained the knife blade. Then he looked up at her, his blue eyes flashing in the moonlight and the spider's web tattoo showing above the neck of his T-shirt, a menacing red spider lurking in its center. He raised the knife but by now she had armed herself with the largest carving knife from the magnetic rack on the wall above the work surface, as well as her pot in the other hand. Above her continued screaming, they could both hear the sound of Willie's footsteps thundering down the stairs, and see the light in the hallway flick on. He turned and ran for the back door, hurling the knife far out into the loch before leaping the rail around the deck and running off along the embankment below.

·   Willie arrived in the kitchen, panting with exertion, to find Lucia still standing against the work surface, still armed with a pot and a knife.

"Lucia!" he cried. "Are you all right?"

"Aye, I...I think so..." she said, then dropped the knife and the pot, flung her arms around his neck and burst into tears.

The ringing phone brought him slowly to his senses and Hamish reached out a languid arm to grab it from the bedside table.

"Hamish, it's me! The bastard's been in our place! He had a knife at Lucia's throat!" Willie's voice was loud, he was breathing hard and he sounded furious.

"Willie?" Hamish was now very much awake. "Is Lucia all right?"

"No, she's no!" Willie shouted. "He threatened to kill her!"

"Who did?" Hamish asked, swinging his long legs out of bed. "Is she hurt?"

"No, but she's in a right state! The Patels are wi' her. It was yon burglar, Hamish, wi' the spider tattoo."

"Willie, where are you?" Hamish put his phone on speaker and grabbed his socks.

"I'm out lookin' for the bastard! And when I find him, I'm goin' to dice an' boil him!"

"Steady on, Willie," Hamish said, pulling on his trousers. "Wait now...did you mean disembowel?"

"I ken what I meant!" Willie roared, and hung up.

Hamish was struggling into his shirt when he dashed out of his bedroom, yelling to Bland.

"James, we've had a—" But before he could say another word, he saw Bland bounding down the stairs.

"Way ahead of you, man," Bland called. "I heard your phone go. What gives?"

"The burglar's hit the Napoli," Hamish said, rushing to catch up with Bland. "This time he's got real nasty."

They piled into the Land Rover with Bland at the wheel, Hamish trying to raise Willie on his phone. At the third attempt, just as they pulled up outside the restaurant, Willie answered.

"Willie, I need you back here, now," Hamish said. "We're at the restaurant."

The restaurant front door was standing open and Lucia was sitting at a table, dabbing her eyes with a tissue and being comforted by Mr. and Mrs. Patel.

"Lucia, I'm so sorry this has happened," Hamish said, crouching beside her. "How are you feeling now?"

"I can't stop shaking, Hamish," she said, another tear rolling down her cheek. "It was awful—and now Willie's out there chasing after that monster!"

"No, Lucia," Bland said, softly. "Willie's here now."

Willie hurried over to Lucia, the Patels moving aside to give him room to hug his wife.

"We can't let this go on, Hamish," he said, his eyes fierce with anger. "Look what he's done to Lucia. We have to catch him!" He stood upright, appealing to Hamish and Bland.

"Let's get back out there—he can't have got far! We'll find him!"

Hamish took a long look at his former colleague. He was wearing a black T-shirt with the Napoli logo on the chest, black cargo trousers and black boots. Swap the Napoli shirt for a Police Scotland one, thought Hamish, and he'd be back in uniform.

"We tried that afore," Hamish said, "and we never even caught a glimpse o' him. He'll have gone to ground again. He must have a bolt-hole somewhere in or near Lochdubh but don't worry—I *will* find him."

"I'll take a scout around outside," Bland volunteered, disappearing out the front door.

"Now," Hamish said to Willie, holding out his hand, "hand it ower."

"What…?" Willie said, innocently.

"You know exactly what I'm talking about, Willie," Hamish said, raising an admonishing eyebrow.

"Aye, okay…" Willie reached into his trouser pocket and pulled out a cylindrical, black, rubber handgrip. Hamish took the grip from him, held it tight and flicked it toward the floor. A telescopic baton shot out of the grip, clicking solidly into place.

"A bit like the one you used to carry as a cop," Hamish said, nodding. He knew Willie wouldn't have gone out after the burglar empty-handed. "But I can't have you running around out there looking for a skull to crack, Willie. In the heat o' the moment, you might just banjo the wrong person wi' this baton. This is an offensive weapon. I could arrest you right now for having this on you."

He stabbed the baton into the floor, retracting it into the handgrip, then passed it back to Willie.

"Put it away," he said. "I never want to see it again. Now, how about some o' your delicious coffee to perk us up while me and Lucia have a wee chat?"

The Patels, dressed in pajamas and dressing gowns, declined the offer of coffee and went home, their shop being a short distance from the restaurant.

"I know it's upsetting having to go through it all again, Lucia," Hamish said gently, sitting down with her at the table, "but let's get it ower wi' while it's all still fresh in your mind. From the beginning—what exactly happened?"

Lucia was running through her story when Bland walked back in, glanced at Hamish and shook his head. There was no sign of the burglar anywhere in the vicinity. Bland gratefully accepted a cup of coffee from Willie while Lucia went on with her story.

"…and then I fetched him a good whack on the side o' his face and he is letting me go. He is looking a bit dizzy, but only for a second. Then he sees his blood on the knife—his blood, not mine—and he gets very angry. He points the knife at me and I am screaming for Willie. His eyes were so creepy and the web tattoo on his neck was so disgusting with that big, red spider in it."

"There was a spider in the web?" Hamish asked. "Are you sure?"

"Of course," Lucia said. "It was red and very nasty. Enough to be making me feel sick."

"Angela Brodie never mentioned a spider in the web," Hamish mused.

"Maybe she never saw enough of the tattoo," Bland suggested.

"Aye, maybe," Hamish agreed. "Go on, Lucia."

"When he hears Willie coming," Lucia said, taking up the story again, "he runs out the back door. You know, where we had coffee the other morning, and he is throwing the knife out into the water. One of the best of my kitchen," she added, with a grimace. "Then he was gone."

Willie took Lucia upstairs, leaving Hamish and Bland to take a look at the deck area.

"We'll likely no' see Lucia's knife again," Hamish said, staring out at black waves flashing moonlit silver crests. "Even when the tide's out, yon's deep water."

"He's a cool customer," Bland said. "He knew the knife would have his DNA from the blood, so he didn't drop it or run the risk of it being found on him if he kept it—he hurled it out there."

Willie came back downstairs with his keys, ready to lock up.

"If you need my help wi' anything, Hamish," he said, "just say the word. I want that spider bastard locked up."

"Thanks, Willie," Hamish said, "but you concentrate on looking after Lucia—leave the burglar to us."

Willie locked the front door behind them and Hamish immediately heard raised voices coming from the main street. He and Bland walked the short distance to where Lochdubh's waterfront cottages lined the shore road to see a group of local residents gathered by the seawall clutching garden tools, cromachs and even the odd shinty stick.

"What's all this about?" Hamish asked, approaching the group.

"We need to protect our homes and property!" came a familiar voice from the midst of the crowd.

"Homes and property!" echoed its twin.

"Aye, this burglar is gettin' right out o' hand!" called one man. "We need to patrol the streets."

"Well, there's only really one street in Lochdubh," Hamish pointed out, "and I'm in charge o' patrolling it. I don't want a gang o' villagers out and about at all hours o' the night ready to lynch any poor passing stranger. Now away back to bed, or I'll arrest the lot o' you for possession o' offensive weapons."

With discontented grumbling, the crowd began to disperse and two small figures were left in the middle, turning this way and that, each time blocked by someone else heading for home. Bounced from pillar to post in tandem like two directionless clockwork toys, the Currie twins eventually stood looking up at Hamish and Bland.

"I'm surprised to see you out at this time o' the morning, ladies," Hamish said.

"Neither my sister nor myself will ever shirk from doing our civic duty, day or night!" Nessie announced.

"Day or night!" Jessie emphasized.

"I'm all for that," Hamish agreed, eyeing the pocket of Nessie's long woolen coat, "although that does rather depend on what you think your civic duty entails. Were you aiming, perhaps, to bake the burglar a cake?"

He reached down and drew a heavy wooden rolling pin from Nessie's pocket, then noticed Jessie, dressed in an identical coat, standing lopsided, with one shoulder and arm lower than the other. He reached down once more, gently lifting her wrist until he could see what was in her hand.

"Michty me," he said, removing a heavy brass knuckleduster from her hand. "That's no' the style o' jewelry I'd expect to see on a respectable lady like yourself."

The two sisters shifted slightly from foot to foot, staring at the ground.

"This is an antique," Hamish said, studying the knuckleduster. "How did you come by it?"

"Our grandfather brought it home when he came back from the trenches in the First World War," Nessie said.

"First World War," said Jessie.

"We use it as a paperweight," Nessie explained.

"Paperweight," Jessie repeated.

"Well, you can put this back in your kitchen," Hamish said, handing the rolling pin to Nessie before turning to Jessie, "and you can put this back on your writing desk. Now away home wi' you and don't let me catch you out here in the middle o' the night armed to the teeth ever again."

The two ladies said good night and, heads bowed, walked off toward their cottage near the church.

"That should keep them off your back for a while," Bland said, grinning.

"Don't you believe it," Hamish said with a laugh. "They'll be nipping my head about something new afore you know it."

"There's a good community spirit around these parts, though," said Bland.

"Aye, but I've never seen them troubled enough to take to the street like that afore," Hamish said, gravely. "This burglar has really got to them. I need to do something about him."

Just then, Hamish's phone rang and Bland could hear the strident tones of a panicking woman on the line.

"Get down here right now, Macbeth!" screamed Mrs. Mackenzie. "They're wrecking my house! They're murdering each other!"

Hamish and Bland ran to the Land Rover and roared off in the direction of Mrs. Mackenzie's boarding house, blue lights flashing but, for the sake of those now trying to get back to sleep, the sirens silent.

CHAPTER SEVEN

If you want to keep a secret, you must also hide it from yourself.

George Orwell, *Nineteen Eighty-Four*

The police Land Rover crunched to a halt on the loose surface of the poorly maintained road outside Mrs. Mackenzie's boarding house. Unlike most of the other houses in the village, where most of the other residents, even those vigilantes who had been patrolling the street, were now tucked up in bed with their windows dark, Mrs. Mackenzie's house was a blaze of light. Every upstairs window shone like a cinema screen in the darkness and figures could be seen staggering past, throttling or walloping each other like some bizarre, late-night Punch and Judy show.

Hamish and Bland dashed into the building and up the staircase where they found the first-floor corridor embroiled in the turmoil of a mini battleground. Two of the bridge crew were wrestling on the floor, and the wooden remnants of what looked like chairs and bedside tables were being launched through the open door of a room on one side of the hallway, in through the open door of its mirror image on the other side in a bedroom-furnishings artillery duel. A man Hamish had never seen before was being held against the wall in a choke hold while flailing against his opponent, another of the bridge crew.

At the end of the corridor sat big Kevin, the digger driver, his head in his hands, yelling above the swearing, yowling, grunting, thumping sound of the battle.

"Cut it out, for Christ's sake!" he shouted. "Have you all gone totally mental?"

Hamish dodged a flying beer bottle, grabbed the one who had the stranger pinned against the wall, slammed him into the opposite wall and slapped handcuffs on him. He then checked on the slightly purple-faced stranger while Bland separated the wrestlers, forcing each of them to sit with the width of the corridor separating them.

"That's enough!" Hamish roared, and the flying furniture ceased. "Out here, all of you!"

The long-range furniture duelists slunk out into the corridor and Hamish found himself facing a ragged, bruised and battered bunch of six combatants, with big Kevin standing, pale and worried but unmarked, at the back.

"You!" Hamish scowled at the stranger. "Who are you?"

"Peter Watkins," said the man in an accent that Hamish identified as Edinburgh, or at least somewhere way to the southeast. "My wife and I are staying in the back room downstairs. I caught this man trying to break into our room."

He pointed at the man in handcuffs, who immediately leapt to his own defense.

"Only because he sneaked into my room and stole my phone!" he cried. "I borrowed a phone, called the number and I could hear it ringing inside his room!"

"I've no idea how it got there..." Watkins croaked, rubbing his neck.

"And what got you two all het up?" Bland asked the wrestlers.

"He put a note under my door saying that he'd shagged my girlfriend!" said the one on the left, pushing himself up off the floor to have another go at the wiry young man opposite. Bland shoved him back down, waving a warning finger at him.

"That wasn't me!" protested the wiry one. "I was just out here seeing if I'd dropped my wallet. Now I think somebody's stole it. Probably him!"

He made to go for his opponent again but Bland stopped him with a warning hand and a dangerous look.

"You're all behaving like a bunch o' bairns!" Hamish scolded them. "You've been spending too much time and too much o' your pay in the pub!"

"Arrest them all!" shrieked Mrs. Mackenzie, heaving herself up the stairs, pausing at the top to gasp for breath and then giving an overdramatic swoon when she saw the mess that was the aftermath of the brawl. "Look at all the damage! Who's going to pay for all this? That's what I want to know."

"They will...I will...I mean, we will. Please, Mrs. Mackenzie," Kevin pleaded, standing at the end of the corridor. "Don't press charges. We can put all this right."

Hamish turned his back on the brawlers and stooped slightly to talk quietly to Mrs. Mackenzie, who pulled her dressing gown tight around herself as if for protection from his words.

"Look at them all," he said, casting a glance over his shoulder. "Every one has bruises to his face, a split lip or a bloody nose, except the big lad that just spoke to you."

Mrs. Mackenzie studied the forlorn faces staring back at her, taking in the superficial scrapes and bashes each of them bore. Only Kevin was injury free.

"Kevin wasn't involved in the fight. He was trying to stop it," Hamish explained. "You see, he's out on parole. If there are arrests and prosecutions, the others might get a wee fine, but big Kevin will likely end up back in the jail. Now that's just no' fair, is it? Why don't I make sure they put all o' this right? You'll end up wi' a few nice new pieces o' furniture to replace the old stuff that got broken and it will all be better than it was afore."

Mrs. Mackenzie looked up at Hamish, looked along the corridor at Kevin, surveyed the battered, exhausted brawlers, and gave a short nod.

"Sort it out, Macbeth," she said, turned and waddled off back downstairs.

"All right, lads," Hamish said, turning to the men. "This is the second stupid brawl I've had to deal wi' in a day, so I'm no' in the mood for any more messing about. Pay attention or I'll chuck you in the jail. Here's what's going to happen, and I'm putting Kevin in charge…"

Once an arrangement for reparations had been outlined and an initial tidy-up was under way, Hamish took Watkins aside.

"You'd best away downstairs and let your wife know you're all right," he said, then he and Bland escorted Watkins to his room.

"Was that guy's phone in your room?" Bland asked him.

"Yes, it was," said Watkins. "He was using a borrowed phone to call his own number and I was woken by it ringing in a drawer. I got up to find it and he burst in, grabbed his phone and hit me. My wife was terrified. I wasn't having that, so I chased him upstairs and then all hell broke loose."

"Very well, Mr. Watkins," Hamish said. "You get back to your wife and we'll have another wee word once everyone's had some sleep."

Hamish and Bland made their way back out to the Land Rover.

"What was that all about?" Bland asked. "High spirits? Too much drink?"

"Aye, both, I should think," Hamish agreed, "plus a few old scores being settled. Right now, I need to get home and write up an initial report on the Napoli burglary, then try to catch some shut-eye afore we have to leave in the morning."

His phone was ringing. A cold chill of dread trickled down his spine. Nobody rang him first thing in the morning, before he'd had a shower, before he'd even had a cup of tea. Nobody except one person, and a call from that person was always going to bring bad news. He lifted the phone, then hesitated, letting another couple of rings go by, then reluctantly pressed the button to accept the call.

"Aye?" was all he said.

"It's on," came the response.

"What is?" he asked.

"The boss has seen yon holiday photos. He reckons he knows where it is."

"How can he be so sure?"

"I don't know. He just knows things, right? He's no' like you. He doesn't go around wi' his eyes shut half the time. He notices stuff, and he says he knows where it is."

"I'm bettin' it's a wild goose chase," he said, sounding more hopeful than confident, making it a bad bet. "A complete waste o' time."

"Well, it's no' like you've got anything better to do, is it? I'll meet you at the usual place. Three o'clock."

"Aye, okay, I'll be there."

He hung up and sat in silence, head bowed, staring at the pattern on the rug, a chain of twisted loops forming a path you could follow for hours but always find yourself back where you started. That was how his life always seemed to go. No matter how hard he had tried to follow a different path, he had always ended up back where he started. Now, however, he had the ominous feeling that things were about to change. The chain was about to be shattered.

Hamish broke the news to Lugs and Sonsie that, yet again, they were to be left at home but tempered it with the fact that Freddy would be popping down to feed them. At the mention of Freddy, the dog's ears pricked up and he cocked his head to one side. Freddy always smelt fantastic. He always smelt of wonderful food and he always provided wonderful treats. All in all, Freddy was probably Lugs's favorite person after Hamish but, as he couldn't really think about more than two people at a time, and because Hamish was always one of them, pretty much anybody could be Lugs's favorite person after Hamish. Yet Freddy, he knew, always smelt fantastic, so he wagged his tail. Sonsie might well have understood that Freddy was to be feeding her today, she might well have understood that Freddy always provided wonderful treats, but if she did, she showed no sign of acknowledging it. And wagging her tail like the idiot dog? Well, that was simply beneath her dignity.

Bland, having managed to clock up more sleep than Hamish the previous night, was to take the first shift behind the wheel while Hamish made a few calls and was climbing into the Land Rover's cab when Elspeth came strolling down the street. She waved a friendly greeting in response to his, then focused on Hamish, standing in the sunshine near the back of the car.

"I came to let you know I'm heading back down south," she said. "I've spoken to your soldier boys and your boss about the army bridge, and interviewed a few locals who...what happened to your head?"

She reached up, delicately outlining the graze where he had been hit by the flying chair in the Hairy Arms.

"Och, it's nothing," Hamish said with a smile. "Just a wee dunt."

"This has nothing to do with the burglar everyone in the village is talking about," she said, her gray eyes turning misty. "This is about something else. This is about death and murder!"

"Whatever your instincts are telling you," Hamish said, gently removing her hand from his head, "I'm no' in any danger, so you've nothing to fret about."

"I'll not fret," Elspeth said, thinking quickly to invent an excuse to extend her stay in Lochdubh, "but if there's murder in the air, then there's a bigger story for me, so maybe I'll hang around a few more days."

"That's up to you," Hamish said, moving forward to the front passenger door, "but if you do, then I'll see you again afore you leave. Right now, we have to get going."

Elspeth watched the Land Rover drive off along the shore road with Lugs at her feet and Sonsie sitting on the gatepost beside her. The big cat, never known for her generosity of affection, sensed a strong affinity with Elspeth, rubbed her face against her arm, purred and looked up into her eyes.

"He doesn't see, does he, girl?" Elspeth said. "The poor man never knows what he's walking into."

Their route took them along the shore of Loch Assynt, heading east into the morning sunshine that cast dramatic shadows over the mountains that dominated the skyline ahead.

"Yon hill is Conival," Hamish said, seeing Bland admiring the slopes from behind the wheel. "It means 'The Joining' or 'Meeting.' It's connected by a ridge on the far side to Ben More Assynt—'The Big Mountain'—which is the highest mountain in Sutherland. Truth be told, it's only a wee bit higher than Conival, which is why you can't see it from down here on this stretch o' the road."

The road wound down into Glen Oykel, following the river of the same name that was fed from the southern slopes of Ben More Assynt. Lower down the glen, the surrounding hills became gradually less dramatically dominant and the river marked Sutherland's southern border. Before long they had reached Lairg, where they turned north on the A836. Cruising through regimented ranks of pine trees, they emerged onto vast areas of moorland reaching out toward hills that were now distant shadows rather than the comfortingly solid peaks that sheltered Lochdubh. Yet by the time they arrived at the scattering of roadside houses at Altnaharra, the mountains had become far more tangible once again and the verges at the roadside acquired low stone walls, always a sure sign that a settlement of some significance lay ahead. Having maintained good speed on the narrow road, Bland slowed as they passed the Altnaharra Hotel.

"A braw place to stay if you like a spot o' fishing," Hamish said, noticing Bland casting an appraising eye over the white-painted building. "Loch Naver's practically in the back garden over there and it's grand for the salmon and sea trout—brown trout, too."

"I'll bear that in mind for my next vacation," Bland said, yawning, still feeling the effects of the previous day. "Right now, we got bigger fish to catch."

"Did you really just say that?" Hamish gave a little shake of his head, as though he couldn't quite believe his ears. "That must be the corniest, crappiest line I've ever heard."

"I know!" Bland laughed. "It just kind of . . . came out before I could stop it."

"You'll hear better jokes in there," Hamish assured him, pointing to their left where a low, prefabricated building boasted walls decorated with colorful murals—the local primary school.

"Yeah, kids love to laugh at jokes, don't they? You ever think about having kids, Hamish?"

"Aye, now and again. I'd like to do it in the right order, though—get married first and then have bairns."

"Is that where Claire comes in? She's one of the calls you're going to make, right?"

"Aye, well, maybe," Hamish said, feeling distinctly uncomfortable. He'd been wondering quite how to fit in a call to Claire without Bland hearing everything. "What makes you say that?"

"I was there when she walked in on you and your 'harem,' remember?" Bland said, laughing again. "Besides, Mrs. Patel told me that everyone in the village thinks you make a great couple. They pretty much count every minute you two spend together. I'm amazed that any agent managed to run a team around here. Everyone seems to know exactly what everyone else is up to."

"It sometimes looks that way," Hamish said, nodding, "but, believe me, there are plenty o' dark secrets hidden away behind cottage doors that the gossips never reach. If I had a penny in my pocket for every secret I've come across, my breeks would be round my ankles."

"Maybe that's how our burglar is managing to stay hidden," Bland suggested. "Maybe he is somebody's dark secret. A relative who's been away. The family secret. The one who turned bad and is now back. Somebody could be hiding him."

"Maybe," Hamish agreed, "but there's no' many around Lochdubh would put up wi' a relative robbing their friends and neighbors. And keeping a secret's one thing—hiding a man in secret is another. Somebody would have noticed something odd if one o' their neighbors had a secret house guest."

Hamish's phone rang and he answered it using the car's hands-free system, even though Bland was driving.

"Sergeant Macbeth," came the caller's voice. "It's me—Joe."

"Aye, Joe, what can I do for you?" Hamish asked.

"Well, I came by your place earlier, but you were gone. I'm no' much o' an early riser, you know. I just thought you'd want to know that I seen him."

"Who did you see, Joe?"

"Well, I seen your pal Willie running past in the street in the middle o' the night. I'd been watching the telly and I must have, you know, nodded off for a bit. He didn't look happy, but he was gone afore I could go out and ask what was up."

"Aye, that's all right, Joe. We know what was upsetting Willie. You'll no doubt hear later but the burglar raided the Napoli last night. Gave Lucia a real fright."

"I heard about that and that's what I need to tell you—I seen him, too."

"Are you saying you saw the burglar, Joe?" Hamish sat forward, suddenly interested. "Where did you see him?"

"In my own back garden!" Joe cried. "After Willie ran past, I took myself upstairs to bed and when I switched on the bedroom light, it shone out ower the back garden, and there he was—squatting down in the middle o' my grass."

"What was he doing there, Joe? Was he hiding?"

"No, he looked like he was cleaning himself. He had what looked like a pack o' yon wipes they use for bairns and he was cleaning his face."

"What happened next?"

"He didn't like the light and he spotted me at the window, so he took off, jumped the back fence and was away. Then I heard you out in the street wi' a bunch o' folk and I thought you'd probably caught him."

"I'm afraid not, Joe, but I'll get him soon. You can count on that."

They said their goodbyes and hung up, Hamish then turning to Bland.

"Weird," was all Bland said at first. "Cleaning himself? Maybe those were some kind of antiseptic wipes. He could have been treating the wound on his face."

"Aye, maybe," Hamish said, rubbing his chin, "but what burglar carries antiseptic wipes just in case he might be whacked in the head wi' a saucepan? It doesn't make sense."

The single-track road drifted along the shore of Loch Loyal, with the slopes of Ben Loyal to their left, and they pulled into passing places from time to time to make way for oncoming vehicles. The road improved and widened only marginally until they were on the coastal plain heading east toward Thurso where there were two lanes and no further need for passing places. On leaving the village of Reay, the presence of the Dounreay facility became apparent by the convergence of power cables suspended from electricity pylons and the site itself soon loomed into view on the coast, the famous white "golf ball" sphere of the reactor building leaving no doubt about the nature of the complex.

A long, straight approach road took them to a security checkpoint where their IDs were checked and their appointment was confirmed by a police officer who had a pistol in a holster strapped to his thigh. His colleague watched attentively, cradling a mean-looking Heckler & Koch automatic rifle. Eventually, they were directed to an office block, outside which a parking space had been reserved for them.

"Armed police in the UK?" Bland said, feigning shock. "I thought British cops didn't want guns?"

"Most of us don't," Hamish said, "and most of the public

don't want to see us armed either. Those two are CNC—
Civil Nuclear Constabulary. They're different to most normal
police. They carry guns."

There was a further ID check before they were met in the
office building by the man they had come to see, who introduced himself as Gordon Wallace. He was middle-aged, with
thinning gray hair and a round, pleasant face. Wallace showed
them to his office and settled them in with a coffee that was
delivered by a young man on his staff.

"So you want to know about Dennis McGill?" Wallace
asked.

"We do, sir," Bland replied. "He's of interest to us in an
inquiry that we're pursuing."

"Very well," Wallace said, with a friendly smile. "I'll tell
you all I can, and you are free to take a look at his file, although
I'd rather that didn't leave my office."

Hamish picked up the file and began sifting through the
sheets of paper in the folder.

"How long did you work with McGill, Mr. Wallace?"
Bland asked.

"We were engineers on the same team for a number of
years," Wallace explained. "We were mainly involved with the
fabric of the buildings—the structure and infrastructure—
not so much the nuclear side of things, although we obviously had to have a good working knowledge of what was
going on here. It's strange that, having worked most of my life
here maintaining, building and extending the place, I'm now
involved in taking it all apart."

"I understand that the whole place is now being decommis-
sioned," Bland said.

"The process is well under way," Wallace confirmed. "It will take decades, but it's all going to disappear, even the big white 'golf ball' that's become something of a local landmark."

"I guess you have to be real careful, given that you're dealing with radioactive materials," Bland said.

"Most of what's left on-site is low-level stuff," Wallace said, "but it needs to be handled properly and, of course, we can't have anything going missing. There's no fissile material here any more—nothing anyone could use to make a nuclear bomb—but anything radioactive could be used by terrorists to build a 'dirty bomb,' so security here is still very tight."

"McGill originally came from Dunfermline," Hamish noted, looking up from the file. "Did you know him before he moved north?"

"No, I only knew him through work," Wallace said. "I come from much further south—Redruth in Cornwall. You can't get much further away from here and still be in the UK!" He gave a little laugh. Hamish smiled politely. "I worked with McGill but we didn't socialize much. He had his family commitments—he was bringing up his daughter single-handed after his wife died—and I had mine. We chatted, of course, and I'd like to think we were friends, although I haven't seen him at all since he retired."

"Seems to me," Hamish said, handing the file to Bland, "that your jobs meant you had to know about all of the comings and goings around here. Scheduling maintenance work would mean knowing what was happening all over the site."

"That's correct," Wallace agreed. "We knew more than most about how Dounreay worked, but a good deal less than some higher up the pecking order."

"Did McGill ever strike you as odd in any way?" asked Bland, browsing the contents of the folder. "From this he seems to have been an exemplary employee, but what do you reckon he was interested in outside of work? Did you ever talk politics, for example?"

"We chatted about all sorts of things," Wallace said, sitting back in his seat and folding his arms, "but he never gave me any impression that he might be any sort of…security risk. Is that what all this is about?"

"We're trying to track down a missing person, Mr. Wallace," Hamish said. "That's all. McGill might be able to help, but now he's proving hard to find as well. Knowing a bit about him could help us track him down, too."

They talked for a while longer before Hamish and Bland were shown out of the building, the CNC officers on the gate watching them drive away. Hamish, who was now behind the wheel, saw one of them talking into the radio attached to his equipment harness, clearly confirming that he and Bland had left the premises.

"Did you notice how Wallace clammed up as soon as he thought we were asking about what you like to call 'cloak and dagger' stuff?"

"Aye, I did that," Hamish confirmed, turning left onto the main road. "I doubt he had any more to tell us, though. He just wanted to make sure he didn't end up saying the wrong thing—which would be anything that might put his job and pension in danger. Anyway, it seems like nobody here suspected McGill of passing information to the Russians."

"I guess not," Bland agreed, "but he is one of the Dozen, so we know that he did. He would have had access to information about the transportation of nuclear material, personnel working at the site and the construction and use of the buildings—all useful intel."

"Well, let's find McGill's place in Thurso and see if we can pick up some 'useful intel' ourselves."

A few miles further east along the coast a scattering of whitewashed modern homes heralded their arrival at Scrabster harbor, and a large, out-of-town supermarket welcomed them to Thurso itself, the most northerly town on mainland Britain. McGill's house turned out to be a bungalow set a few streets back from the sea at Thurso Bay, among a huddle of numerous other, similar houses. It had a bay window to the front room and a neat front garden with a short drive leading to a single garage. The front of the house had been "modernized" by the addition of gray, granite-like stone cladding.

Hamish parked on the street and they walked up the drive, scanning the windows for any signs of occupation. There was no answer when they rang the doorbell, so both men squinted in through the bay window, cupping their hands against the glass to cut out reflection. Inside, furniture had been overturned, drawers had been emptied out on the floor, rugs had been ripped up and the whole room looked like it had been struck by a tornado.

"Phee-ew," Bland whistled. "Looks like the help's got the day off."

"Let's take a look round the back," Hamish said, heading for the side gate between the house and garage.

The rear garden, a flat area of lawn surrounded by rose and shrub borders, was every bit as neat and tidy as the front garden. Unfortunately, the kitchen and dining area were in the same state of disarray as the front room. The back door stood open, splintered wood around the lock telling of a violent forced entry.

"Somebody's given this place a real going-over," said Bland, picking his way up the hall to the front room.

"And this was no tattooed burglar," Hamish added, pointing to some jewelry lying on the floor beside a ransacked photo album. "These would be worth something to somebody…"

"Aye, they would," came a voice from the hall. "My mother. Those are her engagement and wedding rings."

They turned to see a tall, dark-haired young woman standing in the doorway, aiming a double-barrelled shotgun directly at them.

"Take it easy now, lassie," Hamish said, holding his hands in front of him in a calming gesture. "We're police officers. You've nothing to fear from us."

"Aye, right," the woman said with a snort. "I'll make up my own mind about that."

"You'll be Carol McGill, right?" Bland said. "Don't worry, I'm a cop, too." He slowly tapped a finger on the badge attached to his black Police Scotland shirt. "Just visiting from the States."

"We spoke to your friend Jean Graham," Hamish said. He surprised himself by how relaxed he felt staring down the twin barrels and swiftly put it down to the fact that, looking in her eyes, he didn't believe Carol McGill would ever use the gun. "She told us you and your father were in hiding."

The woman relaxed slightly, lowering the gun to point it at the floor, but ready to bring it back into play in an instant. She was wearing combat trousers, a weatherproof jacket and heavy walking boots, with a rucksack on her back. She was clearly prepared for the outdoors.

"So you're the two Jean met," she said. "What are you doing up here in Thurso?"

"Looking for you and your father," Hamish replied, removing his cap, ruffling his hair and jamming the cap back on again, relieved to be out of her firing line. Maybe she didn't want to use the gun, but accidents happen. "We believe Callum Graham was murdered and we want to make sure the same doesn't happen to you and your dad."

"Where is he?" Bland asked. "If we can talk to him and find out who's behind this, we can put an end to it."

"I doubt that," she said, giving him a derisive look. "Dad says we have to take care of ourselves."

"We only want to keep you safe," Bland said. "You can trust us."

"Jean's uncle told her to trust no one," she said.

"Not even the police?" Hamish asked.

"Especially the police," she replied, sneering. "Trust no one except each other is what she said."

"We'll no' sort out this mess that way," Hamish told her. "Tell us where he is and we can help."

"Not a chance!" she said, raising the gun again. "I only came back to pick up some stuff. Push those rings toward me with your foot...slowly."

Hamish did as he was told.

"Careful wi' that thing now," he warned. "We don't want any accidents."

She crouched to scoop the rings off the floor, never taking her eyes or the gun off the two men.

"Now, I have a few things to do out here, so I'm going to close this door," she said, holding the shotgun steady with one hand while grasping the doorknob with the other. "If either o' you two pokes his head out o' this door, I'll blow it right off!"

She closed the door, and they heard her footsteps in the hall.

"What do we do now?" asked Bland.

"We wait," said Hamish with a shrug. "I like my head just where it is."

There was a sudden noise from the front of the house and they looked out the bay window to see the up-and-over garage door opening and hear the bark of a powerful engine starting up. Carol McGill then appeared on a motorcycle, hurtling down the drive. Seconds later, she had disappeared down the street.

Hamish tutted, crossed the room to the door and opened it, tentatively peeking out into the hall. The shotgun was leaning against the wall opposite the front room. He picked it up and snapped it open. The barrels were empty. It was not loaded and, he guessed, it never had been.

"I reckon one thing we've learned from this trip," Bland said, "is that Carol McGill can take care of herself just as well as Jean Graham." He straightened a small painting hanging on the living room wall. It was a watercolor, a little too precise for his liking with a bit too much detail in the landscape and the cottages on the hillside, but it wasn't a bad effort.

"Nice," he said, examining the writing at the bottom. "What does this mean, Hamish? It says 'But An' Ben.'"

Hamish stared at the painting.

"I'd say this was painted by Dennis McGill, wouldn't you?"

he said. "It's all awfy accurate, like it was engineered. A 'But An' Ben' is a two-roomed cottage, although it's no' a term we use up here. It's from the south and east o' Scotland."

"South and east as in Dunfermline?" Bland asked. "That's in Fife, right?"

"Aye, I think Dennis McGill had a wee holiday hideaway, but this painting's no' of anywhere in Fife. I recognize exactly where it is. It's ower near Cromish!"

"Do you think that's where his daughter is heading?"

"No, by the way she was talking, I've the feeling that she's off to join her friend Jean. If I was McGill, I'd have told her to stay well away from me to try to keep her out of danger. Carol McGill will be wi' Jean Graham, but her father will be here!" Hamish tapped his finger on the painting. "We can take in McGill's 'But An' Ben' when we're on our way home."

"Okay, then the next stop on the grand tour is Durness and Kenneth Robb!" He made for the door, stumbling over some debris. "Um...what should we do about all this?"

"I'll make a call once we're on the road and report a break-in," Hamish said. "The local lads will deal wi' this and close up the house."

They retraced their route, heading back along the coast road past Dounreay. As they drove, Bland grew ever more quiet and restless. They had just passed the small village of Strathy when he spotted a roadside inn.

"Pull over here, would you, Hamish?" he asked. "Maybe we can grab a coffee in there."

Hamish did as requested. There were a few cars in the car park, but plenty of spaces. Bland glanced over his shoulder while Hamish swung effortlessly into a marked bay close to an area where wooden benches and picnic tables had been arranged. Bland gave him a dark look.

"We're being followed," he said. "See the dark blue Ford parking just across the way? It tailed us into Thurso and it's been behind us all the way here."

"It wasn't outside McGill's place," Hamish pointed out.

"He picked us up at the end of the street. He'd been waiting out of sight."

"I'll have a wee word wi' him," Hamish said, reaching for his cap.

"He'll take off when he sees you coming," Bland said. "I want to know who he is. Let's do this my way. We'll go inside."

Hamish had to force himself not to look directly at the blue Ford when they got out of the Land Rover and sauntered over to the inn's front door. Bland put on a show of chatting and laughing, explaining to Hamish the intricacies of baseball with lots of animated hand movements. He wanted to make it look for all the world like they were just two colleagues stopping to relax with a coffee.

Inside, a few customers Hamish judged mainly to be tourists sat at tables with drinks and bar snacks. Bland's jolly expression never changed but, out of earshot of the other patrons, he dropped the baseball lecture.

"Looks like we can get a coffee at the bar to take away," he said. "We'll do that and see if he follows us in."

"Who do you think he is?" Hamish asked, standing at the bar where Bland ordered their coffees. "One o' the Dozen? A Russian?"

"No idea," Bland replied, "but he did a pretty good job of staying out of sight when he was tailing us—always at least one car back, two when there was enough traffic. I'd say he's done this before."

"Och, no…" Hamish groaned, a sudden thought occurring. "It's no' one o' the Macgregors' thugs is it?"

"Again, no idea," Bland said, staring intently at the mirror behind the bar, "but he's just walked in, and by the way he's wearing that reefer jacket, I'd say he's carrying."

Hamish glanced in the mirror and saw a tall man with blond hair looking round as though choosing a table. His blue coat was unbuttoned, but Hamish could see nothing inside it other than that he was wearing a white shirt.

"What do you mean?" he asked.

"He has a holster under his left armpit," Bland said quietly. "He's got a gun, Hamish, and I'd bet my ass this one's fully loaded."

CHAPTER EIGHT

I see thou wilt not trust the air with secrets.

William Shakespeare, *Titus Andronicus*

The barman placed their coffees, in takeaway beakers, on the bar in front of them. Hamish paid and they turned to leave, Bland once again making a show of casual, relaxed conversation. Hamish hoped he was smiling and playing his part, but it was all he could do not to take a good look at the blond man, now sitting at a table browsing the menu. He knew if he looked at him and if the man looked back, he wouldn't be able to resist charging at him, even if he did have a gun in his coat. He made it to the door, and they walked outside.

Less than a minute later, the blond man rose from his table and walked to the exit. He pushed open the door, stepped outside and then froze when he was confronted by Bland.

"How's it going, comrade?" Bland said with a huge grin.

Hamish appeared behind the man, pinning his arms. Bland reached inside his coat, plucking a pistol from its holster.

"Cool," he cooed. "Glock 17. I got one just like it at home."

He quickly whipped off his baseball cap, shielding the weapon beneath it while keeping it trained on the blond man. The whole incident took just seconds and there was no one in the car park to see them, but Bland didn't want to take the chance that anyone might witness two police officers holding a man at gunpoint.

"We got our coffees on a little table just over there," Bland said. "Let's have a seat, but you take it real easy now."

Hamish released one of the man's arms but kept the other tightly, yet inconspicuously, locked behind his back. They sat at the table, the blond man opposite Bland, who kept the gun in his hand on the table but still hidden by his cap.

"Who are you?" he asked.

The man carefully raised one finger, pointing inside his jacket.

"My ID?" was all he said.

Bland nodded and the man withdrew a small black wallet from his inside pocket, slowly handing it to Hamish who was sitting at his side, keeping a tight grip on his arm. He flipped the wallet open on the table, then slowly released his hold on the man's arm.

"He's CNC," Hamish said, spinning the wallet round so that Bland could see the badge.

"What are you doing so far from home, buddy?" Bland asked, with something approaching one of his friendly smiles.

"We don't all spend all day guarding the gate," the man replied.

"Sergeant Trevor Marshal," Hamish said, reading from the photo ID card inside the wallet before handing it back to its owner.

"Well, isn't that nice?" Bland said, slipping the gun under the table. "Here we are—all three sergeants together." He released the Glock's magazine clip, checked that the weapon was fully unloaded and slid it across the table to Marshal who quickly slotted it back in its holster, out of sight.

"Thanks for being so discreet," Marshal said. "Americans don't always realize how nervous our civilians can get when they see firearms in public."

"No problem," Bland said, shoving the clip into his trouser pocket. "You can have that back when we're done."

"Why were you following us?" Hamish asked.

"Orders," Marshal said. "My boss didn't like the look of you two, so he told me to keep an eye on you."

"Your boss is Gordon Wallace?" asked Bland.

"No, Mr. Wallace is an engineer," Marshal replied. "He has nothing to do with security. My boss is CNC."

"I'm with your boss," Bland chuckled, reaching for his coffee. "If I was him, I wouldn't like the look of us either!"

"So what were you told to do?" Hamish demanded. "Follow us around and make sure we left the area?"

"That's about it," Marshal confirmed. "See where you went, see who you talked to and see you gone." He had an English accent, which Hamish identified as northern, probably Yorkshire.

"You always been a cop?" Bland asked.

"No, I used to be in the army," Marshal said, then paused, raising one hand slightly. "I have a bottle of water in my pocket. I'm thirsty. Mouth got a bit dry there."

Bland nodded and Hamish tensed, ready to pounce if anything other than a bottle of water appeared. Marshal produced a plastic bottle, opened it and took a swig. In raising it to his mouth, his jacket sleeve rode up slightly, revealing his shirt sleeve with a tattoo creeping out below the cuff onto his wrist.

"Did you get tattooed when you were in the army?" Hamish asked.

"Yeah," Marshal said, with a short laugh. "Probably a few too many times. Some I'd like to get rid of—a girlfriend's name's never a good idea, especially when she runs off with somebody else!"

"You must have seen spider's web tattoos," Bland said. "Any idea what they might mean?"

"That all depends on who's had it inked," Marshal explained. "Nowadays, of course, it could mean nothing at all. Kids have whatever they like the look of—whatever's fashionable."

"Fashions change," Hamish said, "but they're stuck with the tattoo."

"Not necessarily," Marshal argued. "They have pretty convincing temporary tattoos now that the kids can slap on if they're going for a night out, and then clean off in the morning."

Hamish sat bolt upright.

"Clean off?" he asked. "With something like a baby wipe?"

"Maybe not a baby wipe," Marshal said, shrugging, "but a makeup removal wipe—that sort of thing. Why all the interest in tattoos?"

"It's been great talking to you, Sergeant Marshal," Bland said, seeing Hamish beginning to flush with anger. He took a final swig of coffee, adding another sachet of sugar and swirling the beaker before setting it back on the table. "But we got a real busy day ahead of us."

"Aye," Hamish said curtly. "Let's go."

Marshal watched them striding toward the Land Rover.

"Hey!" he called after Bland. "What about my clip?"

"Check out the coffee," Bland replied, pointing at his cup.

Marshal looked down at the table to see his ammunition sitting in the beaker, drenched by the sticky, sugary remnants of Bland's coffee. Every round would have to be thoroughly cleaned before he could reload his Glock.

Hamish pulled out onto the road, accelerating hard. He slapped his hand against the steering wheel, seething with anger.

"Why did I no' see it afore?" he snarled through gritted teeth. "I should have guessed straightaway!"

"You've had a lot of other things to think about," Bland consoled him. "We both have."

"Aye, but how could I be fooled by such a simple disguise?" Hamish raged. "Yon burglar has been having a grand old laugh at us! The tattoo is fake—that's why it was an empty web when Angela saw it but had a spider in it when Lucia saw it. They were two slightly different fake tattoos! The gold tooth will be fake as well, and yon evil blue eyes will be contact lenses."

"You can buy realistic-looking fake tattoos online," Bland said, scrolling through tattoo images on his smartphone, then switching his search to look for colored contact lenses. "And you can pick up packs of cosmetic contact lenses that will change your eyes from brown to blue or pretty much any color of the rainbow."

"He was clever, though, I'll give him that," Hamish said, calming himself and thinking things through. "He created a character that would frighten folk enough for us to believe in him, too. A tattooed psycho wi' evil, wolf eyes. He wanted us spending our time looking for where he might be holed up, or who might be hiding him, when he was actually walking around in plain sight, wi' his tattoo cleaned off and the gold tooth and blue eyes gone. We must even have met the bugger!"

" 'See him but not find him, find him but not see him' was what old Angus said, wasn't it?" Bland recalled.

"Aye, but I'll find the devil now," Hamish vowed. "Lucia did us a big favor."

"Lucia…?" Bland looked puzzled for a moment, and then his eyes twinkled as he caught up with Hamish's train of thought. "Of course—she whacked him with a pan!"

"Aye," Hamish nodded, smiling. "He could scrub off his tattoo and take out his lenses and his tooth, but how do you hide a bruised and cut face? Folk in Lochdubh would be quick to spot somebody in the street or in the pub wi' a bashed face or a keeker."

"Keeker?" Bland asked.

"Keeker—a black and swollen eye," Hamish said quickly.

"You hide in a crowd," Bland said, nodding, "where everyone has a keeker."

"And where does everyone else have a keeker? He's at Mrs. Mackenzie's place," Hamish said. "He went back there last night and started that fight. He knows those lads, so he knew exactly what to do to wind them up into fighting mode. He made sure they all had some kind of injury by setting them all against each other, even the married bloke—although we can't rule him out as a suspect."

"Yeah, we can," Bland argued. "The note that was slipped under the door about the girlfriend. Only another of his mates on the bridge crew would know about the girlfriend."

"That's right," Hamish agreed, trying to visualize the faces of the young men in Stephanie's team. "We can rule out big Kevin. He's the wrong shape to go climbing through windows like our burglar did at the Brodies' house. The disguise wouldn't work on him anyway. You can disguise a lot o' things, but no' your size and shape—and he doesn't have any bruises."

"Then we have five suspects. We should bust in there and search the place as soon as we get back, see if we can find some of the stolen property in one of the rooms."

"Mrs. Mackenzie would go totally doolally if we did that," Hamish said, shaking his head. "She would insist on a search warrant and I know I've no' got enough real evidence to get one. Also, any o' the stuff we found would be useless as evidence if we found it without a warrant."

"So what's your plan?"

"Let me have a wee think about that," Hamish said. "Our burglar's made a right fool out o' me. Maybe I should play him at his own game—deception and lies."

"Just let me know how I can help," Bland said. "Right now, we need to see if we can root out Kenneth Robb in Durness."

"Rooting out" someone in Durness turned out to be a reasonably straightforward business, given that so few people actually lived there. The place itself was not what Bland had expected.

"Durness is different. It's no' like Lochdubh," Hamish advised, driving across the causeway at the Kyle of Tongue. "You'll see once we swing round Loch Eriboll. There's better views there. Prettier than the moors up on this headland."

"How do you mean 'different'?" Bland asked.

"Lochdubh is one village, sitting there by the loch, wi' crofts and cottages here and there in the hills," Hamish said. "Durness is a village, right enough, but it's also a collection o' wee hamlets. It's a bonny place, surrounded by sandy beaches on the Faraid headland. John Lennon used to go there for his holidays when he was a bairn."

Hamish pushed his speed on the empty road toward Loch Eriboll, determined to make up time after their delay at Strathy. He wanted to get their meeting with Robb over as quickly as possible and press on to Cromish to see Moira Stephenson and seek out McGill's place. As always, he longed to get back to Lochdubh, but this time he had an ulterior motive. A plan was beginning to form in his head.

"According to my information," Bland said, consulting notes stored on his phone, "Robb lives in a cottage near the church at Balnakeil."

"Aye, that makes sense," Hamish said with a sigh. "Balnakiel is about as far up the Faraid peninsula as you can bide, no' quite a mile from Durness. Being one o' the Dozen, living there would make it easy to keep an eye on any comings and goings from Faraid Head, where the military have their control center for the firing range ower on Cape Wrath."

On reaching Durness, they motored on past its collection of cottages and guest houses, before turning left for Balnakeil and parking by the graveyard wall. The church itself, surrounded by gravestones, some crumbling and ancient, some looking remarkably modern, was a ruin, its stone walls overgrown with ivy and its roof missing entirely. Bland leant on the wall, peering in at the graves.

"There's been a church on this site for well over a thousand years," Hamish said. "The most interesting grave is inside—a tomb Donald Macleod paid a fortune to have specially built there four hundred years ago. Some say he wanted to make sure his body wasn't dug up and desecrated by his enemies, some say it was an attempt to buy his way into heaven."

"He must have done a lot of bad things in his life," Bland said, "for people to hate him that much and for heaven not to want him."

"Aye, they reckon he was an assassin working for the Mackay clan. He may have killed up to twenty victims and flung their bodies down the waterfall into the depths o' Smoo Cave just down the coast on the other side o' Durness. He believed the Devil lived under the falls, and would take the souls o' the dead in return for making sure he never faced the hangman for the murders."

"Gruesome," Bland said, with raised eyebrows. "Now, where can we find Robb's house?"

Robb's cottage was easy to locate. His name was outside in big letters at the top of a sign advertising trips in his boat from Keoldale Pier to go whale, dolphin and seal spotting as well as the chance to see countless seabirds from kittiwakes and guillemots to puffins and razor bills. They were reading the "Kenny's Boat Trips" notice when the cottage door opened and Kenneth Robb stepped outside. He was a thin man in his late fifties, with a craggy face and unkempt gray hair. He was dressed in a fisherman's sweater, jeans and wellington boots.

"What do you want?" he grunted, locking his front door.

"Well, a trip on your boat sounds awesome," Bland replied, flashing a smile, "but we're really here to talk to you."

"What about?" said Robb. "I need to get down to my boat."

"Mutual friends," Bland said. "Can we come in or shall we do this on your doorstep?"

"Here's fine," Robb said, folding his arms and leaning against his front door as if guarding the entrance.

"How long have you lived here, Mr. Robb?" Hamish asked, a simple question he'd normally ask to set a suspect at ease, although Robb actually seemed uncannily calm, almost as if he'd been expecting them.

"Just about my whole life," Robb responded.

"It's a great spot," Bland said, "with the beach and the dunes on your doorstep. I guess it can get a bit noisy at times, though."

"What do you mean?" Robb frowned.

"I mean when jets and helicopters come screaming along the coast, launching missiles across there..." Bland said, shielding his eyes with one hand and looking out across the Kyle of Durness in the direction of Cape Wrath. "Then there's the naval bombardments from out at sea. Did you know that Cape Wrath is the biggest military live-firing range in the whole of Europe? Of course you did—you've lived here just about your whole life, after all."

"Aye, and I've seen the damage they've done!" Robb snapped, pushing himself off the door to stand upright.

"There's an island off the coast that they've just about blown to bits wi' all their bombs! It should be a peaceful nesting site for all sorts o' seabirds. And the explosions are a nightmare for all the whales. They can hear them from miles away and it confuses the hell out o' them!"

"Right, I get it," Bland said, trying to calm Robb. "You're not a big fan of the pyrotechnics."

"Do you ever travel down south?" asked Hamish.

"Why would I want to do that?" came Robb's response.

"I don't know," Hamish said, with a shrug. "Maybe you visit friends from time to time."

"Sometimes," Robb conceded. "No' that often."

"Have you been down to Applecross recently?" Bland asked.

"No," Robb said, shifting his keys from his right hand to his left. "You're going to make me late..."

"Do the names James Smith, John Martin or William McAllister mean anything to you?" Hamish asked.

"Never heard o' them," was the predictable reply, Robb flicking his keys back to his right hand.

"What about Callum Graham?" Hamish asked.

"Nope, don't know him," Robb asserted, once more juggling his keys. "Now, if you two are done asking stupid questions, I really do need to get down to my boat."

He pushed past them, Hamish and Bland exchanging a look to let each other know they were both happy to let Robb go. They walked back to the Land Rover, Bland gazing out over the water again.

"Cape Wrath looks close," he said. "Almost close enough to swim there."

"You wouldn't enjoy that much," Hamish assured him.

"The water temperature out there doesn't change much, summer or winter—it's ay shocking cold and the currents are fearsome. Also, yon's no' Cape Wrath you can see. It's a complete wilderness called the Parph. Cape Wrath is the northernmost area. There's no roads into the Parph, just a track that runs from the ferry landing stage opposite where Robb's boat is down at Keoldale Pier, up to the Cape Wrath lighthouse."

"How far's that?" Bland asked.

"About ten miles, I'd say," Hamish replied. "Come on—Cromish is no' far. Let's have a chat about Robb on the way."

The road to Cromish took them southwest, skirting the Parph. Hamish stifled a yawn as he drove and stretched his neck.

"You want me to take over?" Bland asked.

"No, I'm fine," Hamish said. "Moira will make us a cup o' tea when we get to her place."

"So what did you reckon to Kenneth Robb?"

"He wasn't in the least bit surprised to see us. Somebody warned him we were coming."

"Yet we didn't tell anyone else we were going to see him," Bland pointed out.

"Aye, but somebody told him to expect a visit at some point—somebody who knows we're sniffing around the spy ring. Who would have done that?"

"Wallace?" Bland suggested. "He knew we were in the area."

"Maybe, but I don't think Wallace is anything other than what he appears to be. He's no' one o' the Dozen."

"Well, whoever it was, we now know they realize we're

tracking them down. That could push them into making a mistake."

"It might. Robb was also lying."

"You spotted it, too. You call it a 'tell' in poker—the keys."

"Aye, when he fidgeted, shifted them from one hand to the other, he was lying. He recognized the names Smith, McAllister and Martin."

"And he knew Graham."

"Aye, and he was down at Applecross on the night of his murder."

"I'd put him as the one who phoned when Graham's car was coming," Bland pondered. "I don't have him down as one of the main team."

"Maybe no'," Hamish said. "Let's see what Moira has to say about him."

Moira Stephenson's cottage sat on the outskirts of Cromish, looking out over Cromish Bay and within sight of its small harbor. The front garden was just as Hamish remembered it from a previous visit some time ago, when he'd had his first run-in with the Russians. He'd prayed then that he'd never have to involve himself in the murky world of espionage ever again, but now here he was, on the trail of spies and murderers.

He enjoyed the scent of the roses lining the path that sloped upward, away from the shore road. It seemed such a peaceful place, certainly not the bustling hub of a murderous spy network, although he was pretty confident that old Moira was no spy, and she was certainly no killer. She looked surprised to see the two men when she opened the door.

"Sergeant Macbeth!" she said with a welcoming smile. "Come away ben and we'll have a cup of something. And who is this you've brought to see me?"

Hamish introduced Bland and they followed Moira through to the kitchen at the back of the house, although she insisted on serving them tea in her front room. They exchanged pleasantries while she prepared the tea and Hamish carried the tray through to her comfortable living room.

"Moira," Hamish said once they were settled, "one of the reasons we're here is that we need your help in identifying someone." He borrowed Bland's folder and slid the peace-camp photo across the coffee table to Moira. Her face turned pale.

"Alex Black," he said. "That's you in the picture, isn't it, Moira?"

She stared at the photograph, studying the slim young woman while running a hand down the wrinkled, sagging skin at her own neck.

"You were Moira Alexandra Black back then, before you married," Bland said, producing another photo. "Do you remember this man?"

Moira gave a little laugh when she held the photo.

"That's yon blithering buffoon," she said. "Blair, his name was."

"He said he used to confiscate cannabis from you," Hamish said.

"Aye." Moira laughed again, covering her mouth as though laughing at such a thing was a disgrace and using cannabis was sinful. "Everybody smoked a bit o' weed back in those days.

Blair made a show o' taking the stuff off me, but he was only taking back a wee bit o' what he supplied!"

"Blair was selling you drugs?" Bland asked.

"Och, no' him himself," Moira said, "but he would send somebody into the camp wi' a supply. He ay had to make it look like the cops were doing their job, so I had tiny amounts seized. That was part o' the deal we had going. We agreed to buy only from his dealer and in return he…" She hesitated.

"Go on, Moira," Hamish encouraged her. "What did Blair do?"

"He…he let us know when there was to be a police raid or when the security services infiltrated one o' their spies into the camp. The spies couldn't be allowed to find out about our weed supply, or anything else."

"What do you mean by 'anything else' and why did they need a spy in your camp?" Hamish asked.

"To see who was there, I suppose," Moira said, slowly adopting a more serious tone. "To see who were friends with each other. To see who talked to each other…"

"And to see who might be trying to recruit you," Bland said.

"Aye." Moira sat up straight, a show of defiance. "There was ay somebody from the other side hanging around as well—ay somebody who said they were working wi' the Soviets. Mostly they were talking nonsense."

"But you came across the real deal," Bland said. "We know that you were paid for supplying information."

"I never sold any secrets, if that's what you mean," Moira said. "I never knew any secrets. All I did was pass on a few names o' people who were sympathetic to the cause."

"The cause?" Bland asked. "Communism?"

"No, not that." Moira waved her hand at him as though swatting the idea. "You can't understand what it was like back then unless you were there. We were all scared. We thought the world was about to be destroyed. We wanted rid of nuclear weapons. We wanted to stop Armageddon! That was the cause!"

"Is that how you got drawn into the spy ring?" Bland asked.

"Spy ring? I never saw it like that. I never knew about a spy ring or a network. I was just small fry."

"Yet you took their money, Moira," Hamish pointed out.

"Aye, and every penny I was given went to funding the cause," Moira asserted.

"Is that how you met Kenneth Robb?" Bland asked. "Was he out to save the planet as well?"

"Kenny was one of us. He cared about the environment and he cared about animals. He had no interest in politics. We didn't really understand what we were getting into. Maybe we still don't."

"Aye, and once they get their claws into you, they never let go, do they, Moira?" Hamish said. "When yon Russian came to your house a while back when he was on the run from us, that was no coincidence, was it? He must have known this was a safe house—that you would help him."

"He scared me half to death," Moira said, a tear welling in her eye. "I really thought he was going to kill me afore he left. Now I've had time to think about it, I suppose I was more use to them alive."

"What makes you think that, Moira? Others have died, you

know," Bland told her. "Chalmers in Glasgow and Graham at Applecross."

"I don't know anything about them," Moira said. "That's the point, you see? Small fry like me and Kenny were never told anything, never met anyone, never knew anybody else's names. He told me once that he'd heard people calling whoever was in charge 'The Boss' and they used to have him running all sorts o' errands. Mainly, though, all we did was pass on gossip. We were told to write down any information we had and leave the notes in secret hidey-holes."

"Dead letter drops," Hamish said, and Bland gave him a nod of congratulations. Hamish shrugged. "I read a spy book once."

"We don't know anything, so we're no threat to them," Moira said, "but we might still have our uses. I think that's why me and Kenny are still alive."

"I think you might be right, Moira," Bland said.

"There's a man called Dennis McGill has a weekend cottage near here," Hamish said. "Do you know him?"

"No," Moira said, shaking her head. "I've never heard of him. Will you have to arrest me, Sergeant Macbeth?"

"That's no' up to me, Moira," said Hamish, looking over at Bland, who gave him a small shake of the head, "but I don't think you've anything to worry about on that score. It's all water under the bridge now, I'd say."

They left Moira and set off in the direction of Scourie, seeking out McGill's cottage on the last leg of the journey home to Lochdubh.

"What will happen to Moira and Robb?" Hamish asked.

"Robb might have been involved in the murder o' Graham, after all, and Moira…well, she might just be 'small fry,' as she puts it, but goodness knows what she's been mixed up wi' ower the years."

"At this point, Hamish, your guess is as good as mine," Bland said. "My orders were to track down everyone on the list and that's what we're going to do. After that, it's out of our hands."

"Well, McGill's place should be just round this corner and…" Hamish took a sharp breath as a silver Audi hurtled past on the other side of the road. "Crivens! He's fairly flying there!"

"Let him go, Hamish," Bland said, and laughed. "We've got bigger flying fish to catch!"

They pulled onto a track leading up off the road to a tiny cottage on the hillside from where there was a breathtaking view out across the Minch toward the Outer Hebrides. The white-painted, single-story building was a low, squat affair that looked like it was hunkered down ready to duck under the bitter winter winds that would soon come howling in off the Atlantic. Hamish needed only a glance to confirm they were in the right place. The shape of the hills to the south and the rock formation near the road had been recorded in faithful detail in McGill's watercolor. Leaving the car at the bottom of the track, they approached on foot, stopping a short distance from the house, anxious not to scare anyone inside into making a run for it.

"Give me a few seconds," Bland said. "I'll cut up to the left and circle round the back."

Hamish agreed, then carried on slowly walking up the track toward the But An' Ben. He had time to admire the pristine, fresh white paintwork on the walls and the solid sky blue on the front door and window frames. That was the proud work of an engineer. McGill clearly wanted to protect his property from the combination of vicious wind, scything rain and bright sunshine that strived relentlessly to strip the paint from every building along the coast.

Judging Bland to be in position, he knocked on the door, which creaked open a crack at his touch. He pushed it open a little further and called inside.

"Hello? Mr. McGill?" he shouted. "It's the police, sir. We'd like to talk to you."

Swinging the door fully open, he dipped his head under the low lintel, stepped inside and gasped in horror. Dennis McGill was hanging by the neck from a low roof beam.

Hamish lunged forward, grabbing McGill's legs and lifting, relieving the short rope's strangling pressure.

"James!" he roared. "Get in here, now!"

James came crashing into the room from the back door and took in the situation with one glance, immediately reaching for his pocket knife.

"Cut the rope!" Hamish yelled, but James was already on it, righting a wooden kitchen chair that was lying on the floor and climbing up to slice through the thick rope. He then helped Hamish lower McGill to the floor, quickly loosening the noose around his neck until he could remove it and cast it aside. Hamish crouched over McGill, feeling for a pulse and holding his face close to the man's mouth, checking for breathing.

Bland stood ready to help, then Hamish looked up at him, a thin smile playing on his lips.

"James," he said, "we're going to have to report a suicide."

☆   ☆   ☆

Elspeth Grant was sitting alone on a rocky ledge near the summit of the taller of the Two Sisters mountains that looked down on Loch Dubh. This was one of her favorite spots. Here she could enjoy the last of the day's sunshine and the view across to the village on the far shore while, as a dedicated news hound, listening via her earpiece for the latest bulletin on the local radio station. She had a few minutes before she had to start her trek back down the mountain path and round the road that led back to Lochdubh's "army bridge."

"Hamish Macbeth," she said out loud, with only herself to hear. "Only you could get the village a new bridge within a day of the Anstey Bridge Disaster. How do you manage these things?"

She smiled, and then frowned. She'd just heard Hamish's name again, like an echo in her earpiece. She'd heard it on the radio!

"Sergeant Hamish Macbeth of Lochdubh police should now be on the line to tell us all about the unfolding tragedy at a hillside location just outside Cromish," the radio news reporter announced. "Are you there, Sergeant Macbeth?"

"Aye...that's right...yes...right here...aye," came Hamish's voice, nervous and hesitant.

"Sergeant Macbeth," said the reporter, "we've had reports of police activity in the vicinity of Cromish and we hear that at least one property is now sealed off with police tape. Can you tell us more about what's happening in Cromish?"

"Aye, well...it's just the one house, actually," Hamish said. "We've sealed off one house due to an...um...incident here."

"Is the incident confined to one property, or should other residents in Cromish be concerned?"

"No, no…not at all. Nobody needs to get into a panic or anything. It doesn't affect anyone else."

"Are you able to tell us what has happened at the house, Sergeant Macbeth?"

"Well, aye…I can tell you that we have recovered the body of a male…a man's body, that is…a dead body…but we're no' looking for anybody else in connection wi' the incident."

"If you're not looking for anyone else, Sergeant Macbeth, can we take this to have been either an accident or suicide?"

"Aye, you can take it like that if you want."

"Sergeant, can you reveal the identity of the victim of this tragedy?"

"No, we've no' been able to…um…inform the relatives o' the deceased yet, so I'm…ah…no' saying anything else at all about that at present and just now."

"Thank you for joining us, Sergeant Macbeth."

"Aye, that's fine and…um…cheerio!"

Elspeth pulled out her earpiece and sat for a second, wide-eyed with disbelief. *Hamish*, she thought to herself, *why the hell are you talking to a radio reporter about a story instead of me? Why are you, the man who doesn't talk to the media, stumbling your way through that interview?*

She blinked and the thoughts changed track. *No*, she reasoned, *that wasn't real. That wasn't the real Hamish Macbeth. The real Hamish never talks to the press and yet you dragged that story out for as long as you possibly could. You made yourself out to be a bumbling idiot. Why did you do that? What on earth are you up to, Hamish Macbeth?*

CHAPTER NINE

Three may keep a secret, if two of them are dead.
Benjamin Franklin, *Poor Richard's Almanack*

By the time Hamish and Bland made it back to Lochdubh, the light was beginning to fade, and he was pleased to see, on driving past the village pub, that Stephanie's bridge crew, who had been set on pulverizing each other the night before, were back to drinking merrily together. They were due to be leaving the following morning, so he was fairly sure they would make the most of their last night in the pub. That would work to his advantage.

No sooner had they parked outside the police station and been treated to Lugs's and Sonsie's customary greetings than Elspeth appeared.

"What was all that about this afternoon, Hamish?" she asked, skillfully embellishing the short sentence with tones of not only disappointment and resentment but also incredulity. "What were you doing giving an interview to a crappy radio station when you always refuse to appear in front of my cameras for a national TV broadcast?"

"It's…complicated," Hamish said, his expression betraying his reluctance to explain.

"So un-complicate it," she said, standing in the police station kitchen with her arms folded and her jaw set.

"Well, that maybe wasn't all it seemed to be…" Hamish said as he finished feeding his pets and tried to give Elspeth his full attention.

"It certainly wasn't you," Elspeth said. "You sounded like a complete numpty, like you didn't have a clue what you were doing."

"That's because he is and because he didn't," Bland said cheerfully, arriving downstairs having changed out of his version of a police uniform into casual gear. "He's exhausted, young lady, so why don't I walk you back up to the Tommel Castle Hotel where you can join me for a late supper? I'll tell you all about how I once wrestled a fifteen-foot crocodile in a blazing desert tarpit when I was in the French Foreign Legion."

"That's utter nonsense," Elspeth said, trying hard not to laugh.

"It's more sense than you're going to get out of him tonight," Bland replied, offering Elspeth his arm. "Shall we?"

Elspeth linked her arm through his and they turned for the door, Elspeth looking back over her shoulder with eyes narrowed for comic effect.

"I'm not finished with you yet, Macbeth," she warned him, wagging a finger.

"No," he said, grinning, "I'll bet you're no'."

Ten minutes later, Hamish stood in front of his bedroom mirror, checking his attire. He wore black running shoes, black trousers, a black sweater and he crammed a black beanie hat over his flaming-red hair. The whole outfit made his lanky legs and long arms look even more awkward and uncoordinated than usual. All things considered, he now decided that he looked less like an overgrown elf and more like a tangle of bootlaces. It would, however, suit his purpose this evening.

He went out the kitchen door and down through his back garden to where a ribbon of trees and bushes stretched along the shore. He would use them to circle round Mrs. Mackenzie's house and get close to the back door without being seen. He made such a proficient job of sneaking silently through the thicket that he rounded one large birch tree only to come across a young sika deer nibbling on a shrub. He stood staring at it and it stared back, appraising him with large eyes like polished black obsidian. It blinked once and they moved past each other, going their separate ways. He was left with the feeling that it understood what he was about to do and had waited there for him to let him know that it disapproved. He shook his head. Weird thoughts had ways of seeping into your mind when you were tired. He needed to get this over with quickly.

The lock on Mrs. Mackenzie's back door was a flimsy affair that wouldn't have kept out a determined toddler for very long and Hamish made short work of opening it. Sneaking through an old scullery into the main ground-floor corridor he almost laughed as he caught sight of himself in the hall mirror, slinking along the wall. He looked ridiculous. His attention snapped back into focus when he heard Mrs. Mackenzie having dinner with her married couple in her small, private dining room.

"I can assure you I've never known anything like that in my house before in all my years in the hospitality business," she asserted. "I blame the police. That Hamish Macbeth is a lazy so-and-so. He's never around when you need him, always mooching around the Italian or up at the Tommel Castle sucking up to old Halburton-Smythe. If you ask me..."

Hamish nodded. He didn't agree entirely with her assessment, but Mrs. Mackenzie's opinion of him had changed not one bit over the years and he was glad he could rely on her consistency. She was now settling in for a good long rant that neither the husband nor his wife would dare cut short, so now was a good time to take a look in their room. The door opened at once, having been left unlocked.

The large rear bedroom was actually only a very slightly bigger version of the upstairs bedrooms, with a double bed instead of a single. The curtains were drawn and he pulled a flashlight from his pocket rather than switching on the ceiling light. It was unlikely that any useful illumination would penetrate down through the layers of dead moths and wasps lining the light's glass bowl in any case.

He scanned the room with his flashlight. Above the bed was a framed, faded and yellowing image of an angel bathed in light and looking up to heaven. Beneath it was the proverb: "Charm is deceptive, and beauty is fleeting; but a woman who fears the LORD is to be praised."

Hamish quickly checked the couple's baggage and rucksacks, the cupboard and the bedside cabinets. He found nothing out of the ordinary save for a small clingfilm wrap of cannabis resin. He put that back in the sock drawer where he had found it. After an evening with Mrs. Mackenzie, they'd need a smoke up in the hills tomorrow.

Making his way upstairs, he was impressed by how well the lads had tidied up. As far as he could tell, everything was spic and span. Most of the door locks opened with no more than a decent shove and he found nothing in the first three rooms he checked save for stashes of booze and some colorful reading material of which Mrs. Mackenzie would definitely disapprove.

The fourth room seemed no different. As with the others, he left the room light off, using only his flashlight. He had finished checking all the obvious places and was about to leave when his torch beam picked out something on the carpet next to the wardrobe. He bent down to examine it, rubbing it between his fingers. It was a trace of white dust—plaster dust by the feel of it. Was this battle damage that the clean-up crew had missed? That seemed unlikely. It was in an odd place, between the wardrobe and the outside wall, surely an area that would not have been affected by the brawl. So how had it got there? Had it fallen from above?

He tracked his light up the wall and it settled on an air vent. The standard of décor in the house generally ranged from shabby down to virtually decrepit, but there were scratch marks around the small plaster grille that looked new. Hamish reached up and gripped the grille. It was loose. He pulled it away from the wall, then reached into the recess, retrieving a rolled plastic carrier bag.

He glanced out of the window. There was no sign of the

lads arriving home from the pub just yet. Doubtless he would hear them before he saw them. He unrolled the bag, opened it wide and shone his light inside. Bingo! There were rolls of cash, jewelry, a pack of blue contact lenses and sheets of web tattoos. He had found his burglar! Rolling the bag as it had been before, he replaced it in the vent and refitted the grille.

Slipping his torch back into his pocket, he crept out into the corridor, thinking hard. It would be easy enough to find out whose room that was, but simply arresting him might end up betraying the fact that he had broken into the boarding house. Having used illegal means to find the evidence, his case against the burglar would be thrown out of court. He needed more than just the bag of goodies from the vent. He had to catch the burglar with the loot in his possession.

What he needed was…he froze. The muffled voices from the dining room had suddenly grown louder. The door was open and the couple were heading to their bedroom. There was a clatter of crockery, the squeak of trolley wheels and the shuffling of feet—Mrs. Mackenzie was taking the dinner dishes to the scullery, blocking his way out. Then, with horrifically perfect timing, he heard singing, laughing and chanting from outside—the lads were on their way home.

He risked a glance over the balcony and, in the mirror, saw Mrs. Mackenzie disappear through the scullery door. He had to move fast, trotting down the staircase before vaulting the banister into the hall. Cursing himself for landing with an annoyingly loud thud, he bounded three paces into the dining room, hugging the wall, out of sight, when he heard Mrs. Mackenzie calling.

"What was that?" she yelled, emerging from the scullery. "Is that you drunken heathens trying to frighten an auld lady? Well, you'll have to try harder than that!"

She came marching up the hall and Hamish skipped across the dining room, hiding behind the floor-length curtains. A moment later she was at the dining-room door.

"Is somebody in there?" she cried, poking her head round the door. "You'd better show yourself or I'll…"

Whatever she might have done was left unsaid when a barrage of knocking and hammering came from the front door, accompanied by drunken pleas from the bridge crew to let them in, solemn promises that they would behave and never be late back again, and hysterical laughter.

"Wheesht!" hissed Mrs. Mackenzie. "You'll wake the whole o' Lochdubh wi' that infernal racket! I'm coming!"

She waddled to the front door, fishing her keys out of an apron pocket. Hamish took advantage of the infernal racket to heave open the dining room's sash window and jump out into the overgrown back garden, racing for the cover of the woods. *Yon sika couldn't have covered that ground faster,* he told himself, standing panting with his back to a tree.

Once back in his kitchen, he collapsed into a chair, pulled off his beanie and grabbed his phone.

"Silas?" he said when his call was answered. "Aye, it's me. I know it's late but I guessed you'd still be up, what wi' this burglar around. The thing is, I might need a wee bit o' help from you and Freddy tomorrow. We'll put an end to our burglar's game, and we can have a wee bit o' fun later on into the bargain. You're up for it? Good lad—I knew you would be. I'll be ower to see you in the morning."

✳ ✳ ✳

When Stephanie Gibson pulled up in her minibus outside Mrs. Mackenzie's house the following morning, her six passengers were spilling out the front door, a couple still looking the worse for wear but the rest buoyed by the greasy fry-up their landlady had provided for breakfast. They traveled light, most having stuffed everything they'd needed for the week into a small holdall or an even smaller rucksack.

A couple of minutes later, they were all aboard, laughing, crying mock tears and waving to Mrs. Mackenzie, who watched them go from behind the net curtains in the safety of her front room. There were calls for a halt at the Patels' mini supermarket on the way out of town, where they stocked up on snacks and fizzy drinks for the journey before Stephanie finally got them all back in the minibus and on the road to the bridge. She rounded a bend and entered the lane of traffic cones that directed vehicles away from the old bridge to the army bridge, but pulled to a halt again before she could cross the Anstey, Hamish's police Land Rover blocking the way.

"What now?" she tutted, frustrated by yet another delay.

She climbed out of the minibus and strode over to where Hamish stood by his car alongside Bland, who had Lugs on a leash.

"What's up, Hamish?" she asked. "Is there something wrong wi' the soldier boys' wee bridge?"

"No, no, it's fine," Hamish replied. "I just wanted to have a wee word wi' your lads afore they leave town, just to thank them on behalf of Lochdubh."

"All right," she agreed reluctantly before turning back to

the minibus. "Come on, boys—everyone out! Sergeant Macbeth has something to tell you!"

With a chorus of moans and groans, her crew piled out of the minibus, assembling in a bunch in front of Hamish and Bland. Some carried their rucksacks, prepared to head for a picnic table in the morning sunshine and start consuming their travel supplies if there was to be any sort of holdup.

"Thanks for humoring me, lads," said Hamish with a big smile. "I just wanted to thank you for all your hard work this week. You did a grand job clearing the rubble out o' the river and getting the bridge ready to be fixed. Everyone in the village is happy to have had you here, especially the landlord in the pub!"

There was a cheer and a burst of laughter.

"Mrs. Mackenzie wasn't quite so happy wi' you," Hamish went on, "but even she was impressed wi' the job you did tidying up her place and she's looking forward to the arrival of the bits and pieces o' furniture you ordered online for her.

"Lochdubh is grateful for what you've done and you can all be proud o' what you've achieved here. Give yourselves a round o' applause, lads."

Hamish led the clapping and everyone joined in, the bridge crew highly amused to be congratulating themselves.

"There's just one more thing," Hamish added, calming the clapping. "As you know, we've had a burglar active in Lochdubh while you've been here. No doubt you heard all about him in the pub. He has a spider's web tattoo on his neck…" Hamish dragged his fingers down the right side of his neck to indicate where the tattoo was. "…blue eyes and a gold tooth. If any o' you come across him wherever you next end up working, give me a call straight away. He's dangerous, and I know you're all fit and up for a ruck, but don't approach him—just phone me. I'll likely have him under arrest soon enough anyway."

"Bollocks!" came a cry from the crew. "You'll never catch him!"

"Aye, but I will," Hamish assured them. "We've just recovered some vital evidence." He held up a clear plastic bag containing a large kitchen knife. "Sergeant Bland and myself have been doing a spot of fishing in the loch wi' this…" He held up a big red horseshoe magnet with silver ends. "This is one of a set of powerful magnets we use for underwater searches. Using the search apparatus, we located this kitchen knife that was used by the burglar when he raided the Napoli. He threw it in the loch. We know it has his blood on it and, although you can't see any now, the water in the loch won't have washed it away completely. We'll be sending this off to the forensic lab in Strathbane and they'll be able to extract his DNA from the traces of blood. We also have this…"

Hamish held up another clear plastic bag, this time containing a banknote.

"After he'd been in folk's homes, we were a wee bit worried that the burglar might try the Napoli, so all o' the notes in their cashbox were sprayed wi' a chemical agent. To us, it's invisible and odorless, but to specially trained sniffer dogs like Lugs here, it reeks o' venison sausages."

At the mention of venison sausages, Lugs began barking.

"What's the matter, boy?" Bland asked, holding the leash taut. "You smell some venison sausages?"

Lugs barked again and Bland allowed him to pull on the leash toward one of the bridge crew.

"Sorry, buddy," Bland apologized. "He's only supposed to do this when he gets the scent of venison sausages."

Lugs began barking again.

"Do you mind if I ask," Hamish said, stepping forward to stand near the wiry young man, "if you have anything in your rucksack like venison sausages?"

Lugs barked even louder.

"No," the young man said, shifting the bag nervously on his shoulder. "I don't."

"Well, there's got to be something in there making the dog act like this," Bland said. "It would be good if we could take a look just to see what else might make him act like he's smelt venison sausages."

Lugs started barking madly and the young man's eyes flared with anger. He flung his bag at Hamish, then turned and ran. He got no more than five steps when Silas and Freddy appeared from behind the minibus, blocking his way. He skidded to a halt and immediately felt Hamish grab hold of him, wrenching his right arm behind his back.

"Because you are exhibiting suspicious, aggressive, even downright violent behavior," Hamish said in his ear, "I've decided to make you the subject of a 'stop-and-search.' Bring this gentleman's rucksack ower to yon picnic table, would you, Sergeant Bland?"

Hamish marched his suspect over to the picnic area and ordered him to stand leaning forward with his hands on a table.

"What's your name, laddie?" Hamish asked, patting the man down.

"I'm sayin' nothin'!" snarled the young man.

"How about we try you with Craig Evans?" Bland said, pulling a driving license photo card from a wallet he'd just found in the rucksack, then riffling the notes slotted inside. "You're carrying quite a lot of cash, Craig. How did you manage to keep hold of so much after spending every night this week in the pub?"

Evans simply glowered at him.

"Anything sharp in your pockets that might jab me?" Hamish asked, receiving no response before going through the pockets of Evans's jacket and jeans.

"What you got in here, Craig?" Bland asked, hauling a rolled carrier bag out of the rucksack. He carefully emptied the contents of the bag onto the picnic table and wads of cash bounced out along with a selection of rings, earrings, a couple of watches and the paraphernalia of the tattooed burglar disguise.

Evans suddenly levered himself upright, swung his right arm round to batter Hamish aside and made to run off. Hamish stuck out a long leg, tripping him. Evans sprawled on the picnic area grass and had almost sprung to his feet again when Hamish clamped a hand on the back of his neck. Yanking him roughly upright, he spun him round, grabbed him by the throat and forced him back against the table. There came a gasp and some murmuring from the rest of the bridge crew. Hamish gave them a menacing look that immediately silenced them.

"You lot bide right where you are!" he snarled, then spoke quietly to Evans so that only he and Bland could hear. "You scared the wits out o' two very good friends o' mine. They'll be having nightmares about you, Evans, wi' your silly disguise.

Thought you were so clever, didn't you? But you're no' that smart at all really. We fooled you wi' a fresh knife that I borrowed from the Napoli's kitchen and a child's toy that I bought in Patel's this morning.

"As for Lugs"—the dog looked up adoringly at Hamish, wagging his tail at the mention of his name—"he's no' had any special training. He ay barks when he hears the words 'venison sausages.'"

Lugs barked and Hamish reached into his pocket, pulling out a sausage as a reward for his faithful hound. Evans tensed, sensing a moment of distraction, ready to lash out at Hamish again, but there came a quiet "click" and he looked down to find himself handcuffed to Bland.

"We fell for the disguise, but you fell for the bluff!" Bland grinned. "You lose, buddy!"

"Is that him?" roared a voice from the road and Willie came thundering toward them. "Is that the bastard that had a knife at my Lucia's throat? Let me at him!"

Freddy and Silas quickly caught hold of their friend, slowing his charge until Hamish was able to help them calm him down.

"Take it easy, Willie," he said. "I can't let you 'dice an' boil' anybody, can I? I'd have to lock you up and that would leave Lucia to cope wi' the Napoli on her own. You don't want that, do you?"

Willie stopped struggling but his eyes flared with fury again when Bland walked Evans over to the Land Rover.

"You better no' set foot in Lochdubh ever again!" he yelled at Evans. "People round here have got long memories! They'll want restribulsion!"

"You heard him," Bland said to Evans, shoving him into the car, "and that didn't sound good, whatever he said."

With Evans locked in the holding cell at the police station, awaiting transportation to Strathbane, Hamish left Bland in charge, driving over to Braikie to visit the hospital. He had always liked Braikie, mainly because it was so different to Lochdubh that the two couldn't be compared. Braikie was a market town with a small cluster of Victorian buildings at its center and a pretty little inland loch on its outskirts, near the railway station that was its main link to the outside world.

Braikie's hospital, however, was not one of Hamish's favorite places. A few minutes pacing its polished linoleum corridors beneath the soporific lighting made him lose track of time and start to wonder whether it was morning, noon or night. Whatever time of day it was, the smell of disinfectant, floor cleaner and hand sanitizer never slept. It stayed with him for days. He reckoned it permeated the hairs in his nose.

In the Accident and Emergency department, he and his friend Mike, a doctor at the hospital, bumped into each other. They stood for a while chatting outside a row of curtained treatment booths.

"Listen, Mike," Hamish said, "about our little arrangement...I can't tell you how awkward it would be for me if anyone was to find out."

"I understand, Hamish," Mike said, slapping his pal on the shoulder. "Don't worry, I'm not saying a word to anyone."

"Good, I'll be making a move again soon, likely today."

"Good luck with that. Now, if Claire's back on the market, I might want to make a move there, too."

"Who says she is?"

"I say," Mike said, laughing. "I heard a wee story about her catching you with three other women in a hotel!"

"Where the hell did you hear that?" Hamish said, shaking his head. "When folk gossip like that, stories get distorted. I wasn't actually there wi' three women. There were three women there wi' me, but..."

"Don't try to wriggle out of it, Hamish! Whatever happened, everyone knows Claire's sorely pissed off with you. I'd be willing to bet fifty quid that I can get her out on a date before you can."

"Fifty quid?" Hamish sounded shocked. "I thought you doctors were ay complaining about being underpaid. Now you're willing to throw away fifty quid?"

"So you'll take the bet?"

"Like hell he will!" One set of booth curtains was flung open and Claire stood there, in her paramedic uniform, bristling with fury. Her eyes were moist with angry tears. "You pair really are the limit! I came in here to settle a patient we'd just picked up..." A nurse stood behind Claire in the booth, tending to a patient in the treatment bed. She looked out at the two men, shaking her head. "Then I hear you two talking about a 'little arrangement,' talking about me being 'back on the market'—even placing a bet on who can get to me first? Well, listen in, because here is the news—you can both bugger off!"

Claire stormed off toward the ambulance bay. Mike gave Hamish a look of hopeless embarrassment, then said, "I've... er...got some charts to check," and vanished in the opposite direction.

Hamish looked after Claire and decided that, even if it was just to clear his conscience, he had to talk to her. He caught up with her by her ambulance, checking her emergency bag.

"Claire," he said, approaching slowly.

"Are you still here?" she answered. "I thought I told you to—"

"I know all that sounded bad, but I can explain."

"Go on, then!" She turned to face him. Her eyes were red. She'd been crying. "This better be good."

"What you heard about 'the arrangement' was nothing to do wi' you—I swear."

"So what was it all about then—you 'making a move'?"

"Not you. I can't talk about that yet, but I'll be able to tell you all about it soon."

She stared up at him, straight into the big Highlander's sad, apologetic, honest face.

"There's still the matter o' the bet!" she snapped, as though suddenly remembering. "I don't know if you'd noticed, but I'm no' a racehorse or a bloody greyhound!"

"I didn't take his bet, though, did I?" Hamish pleaded his innocence. "I was as shocked as you were when he said that. Well...maybe no' quite as shocked and upset as you...I mean...you were hearing it about yourself and..."

"Och, shut up, Hamish, afore you make things worse."

"I'd far rather make things better. Why don't we rearrange dinner at the Napoli? I know your shifts—you must be off tomorrow night, right? We'll share a bottle o' Willie's Valpolicella and—"

"I'll think about it," she said, pushing him gently away with a hand in his chest. "Now I've got work to do, so get lost."

Hamish walked back into the hospital, mulling over their conversation and deciding that he had grounds for some confidence. After all, he reasoned, "get lost" was definitely a step up from "bugger off."

By the time Hamish arrived back in Lochdubh, Craig Evans was in a police van on his way to a cell in Strathbane and a date in court. Bland had called Hamish to let him know Evans had been picked up and now sat waiting in the kitchen, as Hamish had asked him to, dressed not in his version of the Police Scotland uniform, but in a neat gray suit with a white shirt and blue tie.

"That's a braw suit," Hamish said. "I knew you'd have brought one wi' you."

"I kind of had to," Bland said. "Sometimes there are people I have to meet where that Chicago Police uniform wouldn't... well, it wouldn't be appropriate."

"Aye," Hamish said, smiling, "and maybe because you're no' really a Chicago Police officer at all."

"I've told you before," Bland said, laughing, "I am and have been many things. The main thing is, you and I are on the same side. Now, what's this plan you've come up with?"

"I'll explain up at the hotel," Hamish said. "We'll need their help as well. Make sure you bring yon letter wi' you—the one from the Home Office."

At the Tommel Castle Hotel, Silas showed them into a room that was part of the office suite, furnished with a long boardroom table surrounded by chairs. Colonel Halburton-Smythe then appeared, followed by Priscilla and Freddy.

"What's this all about, Macbeth?" barked the colonel. "I hear you've already commandeered two of my staff today."

"Aye, Silas and Freddy were a grand help this morning," Hamish acknowledged. "Thanks again, lads."

"Are you giving our brave boys medals?" Priscilla teased, tweaking Freddy's cheek before taking a seat.

"No, but a show of medals might help, actually," Hamish said, thinking ahead. "Do you still have your old army uniform, Colonel?"

"Of course," the colonel replied. "I have two, counting my mess dress."

"Ooh, are we all dressing up?" Priscilla asked, laughing, clearly in one of her more frivolous moods. Hamish frowned at her.

"Aye, in a manner of speaking..." he said.

"Now look here, Macbeth," the colonel interrupted. "Just get to the point. We're all busy people. Freddy has prep to do in the kitchen, Silas is working on next week's duty rosters and..."

Bland slid the Home Office letter across the table to the colonel.

"It's a matter of national security, sir," he said. "In reading this, I'm obliged to remind you all that you are forbidden from discussing with anyone else anything that may happen here today, under the terms of the UK Government's Official Secrets Act."

The colonel's eyebrows pricked up and his back straightened as his sense of duty kicked in. He barely glanced at the letter beyond the Home Office crest.

"In that case, gentlemen," he said, "we are at your service."

"Fine," Hamish said, "here's the plan..."

The Jacobite bar had very little in common with Braikie's hospital. It was neither spotlessly clean nor determinedly disinfected but one of the qualities they shared was the way the lighting isolated visitors from the progress of time in the world outside. With no sunlight, or moonlight, or proper darkness, just a constant level of, in the case of the Jacobite, unchanging gloom, it was as if time stood still. The two men sitting drinking in their usual alcove couldn't care less what time of day it was. This was their refuge—the only place they ever felt safe.

"Did you hear him on the radio—yon eejit cop?" asked one, taking a swig from his beer.

"Aye, he sounded a right bampot," said his drinking partner, a heavy-set man, more robust than his friend.

"He fell for it though, right? We're in the clear."

"For now. We'll never be clear o' this business. The boss will ay be after us for somethin'."

"What else could he want?" said the first man, rubbing a hand across his forehead. "We've done everythin' he's asked o' us, and more besides. I'm no' sure how much more o' this I can take. I'm too old for all this. I just want—"

"Och, shut your stupid trap!" snapped his friend. "If the last few weeks have taught us anything, it's that we can't hide from the boss. He knows stuff. He knows how to find folk. He'll always be able to find you or me, no bother at all. So don't go bleatin' on about how you can't take any more, because we've just got to do as we're told. Otherwise, we'll end up like McGill!"

"Aye, and the others...but where will it all end? He says he doesn't like loose ends. What loose ends can possibly be left?"

"There's the two women—Graham's niece and McGill's daughter."

"He'll no' want us going after them, will he?"

"You two are no' going after anyone ever again." Hamish stood blocking the alcove, staring down at the two men. One of them made a move to stand and slip past him but Bland stepped out of the shadows, a threatening figure in his suit, now accessorized with dark glasses. Hamish sat down at the table, blocking in one of the men, while Bland did likewise with the other.

"Who the hell are you?" asked the first man.

Hamish pointed out his uniform, taking off his cap to set it on the table.

"Obviously I'm a policeman," he said. "Sergeant Bampot Macbeth."

"You're the one that found the suicide," the heavier man said.

"Aye, except it wasn't a suicide, was it, lads?" Hamish said.

"That's what you said on the radio," the first man said, nervously.

"But that wasn't exactly the truth, was it?" Hamish said.

"How should we know?" said the larger man.

"Because you were there. You set it up to look like suicide," Hamish said.

"No! We never did!" cried the smaller man. "You've got that all wrong."

"I don't think so," Hamish argued. "I have it on good authority that you two strung up Dennis McGill."

"Who says so?" demanded the heavy man.

"He does," Hamish said, pointing to a man Bland had just waved over to join them. His face looked bruised and puffy and he was wearing a neck brace but the two men recognized him instantly. "I think you know Dennis, don't you, lads?"

The smaller man reacted, pushing himself away from the figure of McGill as though he'd seen a ghost, scrabbling deeper into the alcove and knocking over his beer as he did so.

"Och, now look what you've done," Hamish complained, picking up his cap and brushing beer off it. "Just bide still, will you?"

"It said on the radio he was dead!" said the heavy man.

"Aye, but you can't always believe what you hear on the radio," Hamish pointed out. "On the other hand, I'm beginning to believe everything I hear from Mr. McGill. He can't talk much right now—he's got a bit o' a sore throat—but he did tell us where we would find you two scumbags."

"Are you going to arrest us?" the small man asked.

"Och, no," Hamish said, a note of mock cheerfulness in his voice. He pointed at Bland. "I'm no' the one who'll be arresting you. That will be up to my American friend here."

"Howdy," was all Bland said.

Hamish stared at him, a slight frown on his brow.

"We will, however, be taking you somewhere safe," he said, "and after that you might be taking a wee trip across the Atlantic."

"America?" wailed the small man. "I don't want to go to America."

"Come on, now," Hamish said. "New York? Niagara Falls? Los Angeles? Disneyland? Who doesn't want to go to

America? Sadly, you won't be seeing any o' that sort o' thing on your trip."

He pulled out his handcuffs, cuffed the two men to each other and led them outside, loading them into the Land Rover. Bland helped McGill into the colonel's Range Rover— borrowed for this special mission—then stood with Hamish in the Jacobite's car park.

"'Howdy'?" Hamish said, laughing. "I'd have thought I could trust an American secret agent to play an American secret agent better than that."

"I was being menacing," Bland said, grinning.

"That all went better than I could have hoped," Hamish said. "I was feared they might cause a scene and make a run for it."

"Just as well they didn't," said Bland. "I couldn't see a thing in there wearing these sunglasses."

"Right," Hamish said, producing his car keys from his pocket. "I'll take my two back to the Tommel Castle. You take Mr. McGill back to the hospital. Mike wants to keep an eye on him. See you back at the hotel."

CHAPTER TEN

We two have paddled in the stream,
From morning sun till dine,
But seas between us broad have roared
Since auld lang syne.
                    Robert Burns, "Auld Lang Syne"

Elspeth sat on the patio outside the main bar at the Tommel Castle Hotel, sipping tea from a china cup, enjoying the afternoon sunshine and the view over the loch, and wondering whether she should have headed back to Glasgow by now. The story about the bridge had been sweet, the kind of cute and uplifting story they liked to tag on at the end of the news show, and it was always good to be back in the area, but all the real action was down south. That's where the big stories broke. She saw Hamish's police Land Rover pull into the car park and made to wave to him, but he was taking no notice. His mind was clearly somewhere else and when he dragged two handcuffed and hooded men out of the car, marching them briskly to the hotel's side entrance, her mind immediately wanted to be wherever his was.

She was about to rush inside to find out what was going on when the colonel's Range Rover roared into the car park and Bland jumped out of the driver's seat wearing a suit. He, too, then rushed to the side entrance. What the hell was going on? Elspeth pushed her tea aside and marched into the hotel. She spotted Priscilla crossing the bar wearing a very business-like suit. Priscilla always looked smart, she mused, but usually more elegantly casual. She didn't seem herself.

"Priscilla!" she called, waving. Priscilla paused, a slightly pained expression on her face as Elspeth trotted over to her.

"Sorry, Elspeth," she said, "I don't have time for a chat right now."

"What's going on?" demanded Elspeth. "I've just seen Hamish bring in two men in handcuffs with bags over their heads!"

"You'll have to ask Hamish," Priscilla said, her eyes flitting nervously left and right. "I need to be somewhere else right now." And she hurried off.

Elspeth watched her go. Priscilla headed for the stairs, trotting up them as fast as her high heels would carry her. That wasn't a bit like Priscilla. She generally glided around the hotel as though she were walking on air, as though she owned the place, which she did, or one day would. Priscilla didn't rush around like a panicked minion summoned by an intolerant boss—she was usually the one doing the summoning.

Crossing into the reception area, she found the hotel manager, Mr. Johnson, behind the reception desk.

"Good afternoon, Miss Grant," said the manager. "Are you able to say how many more nights you might be staying? It's just that I'm having to juggle our room allocations at the moment."

"Tonight, at least." Elspeth frowned, then added, "Possibly tomorrow. Something weird's going on, Mr. Johnson. People are acting strangely."

"I know," Mr. Johnson said with a troubled sigh. "For some reason the colonel has booked out the entire second floor. I need two of those rooms this evening."

"The second floor?" Elspeth asked. He nodded and she walked over to the stairs, heading for the second floor. She'd reached the landing above the first floor when she saw Hamish at the top of the stairs, talking to Freddy, who was also wearing a suit, dark blue as opposed to Bland's gray.

"Freddy," she said, continuing up the stairs, "you look very smart. What's the...?"

Freddy smiled, waved and disappeared along the corridor without saying a word. Elspeth carried on up the stairs, Hamish stopping her at the top.

"Hamish, if I have to ask one more time what's going on," she said, "I'm going to scream—and don't tell me it's complicated."

"More complicated than you'd ever believe," Hamish said, "but I promise that, once it's all over, I'll give the whole story exclusively to you."

"Not to some crappy radio station?"

"That," Hamish said, "was a means to an end. The reporter owed me a favor—I let him off a speeding ticket—so he let me talk like an eejit on the radio."

"This gets more intriguing all the time," Elspeth said. "You'll give me the story on camera?"

"Don't push it. You'll never be able to broadcast this."

Bland came strolling over from further along the corridor.

"Why don't I handle this, Hamish?" he said, reaching into his pocket. "You best check they're all ready. Let's take a seat, Elspeth."

He showed her his Home Office letter, gave her his spiel about the Official Secrets Act, at which she rolled her eyes, and started to explain.

"Hamish has set up a sting," he said. "He's got two guys for attempted murder, but we need some information from them."

"That's what police formal interviews under caution are all about, isn't it?" Elspeth pointed out.

"Yeah, but these two will just clam up if we go that route, and we need to move quickly. They're too scared of their boss to say a thing. We want to shake them up a bit—maybe make them more scared of us than they are of him."

"Well, if I can't report on it, then I want to be part of it," Elspeth said.

"I don't see why not," Bland said. "Get into your most formal work outfit and you can hang out with Priscilla."

"We're ready," Hamish said, walking back toward them. "The big lad's first up. We'll let the smaller one sweat awhile longer."

Hamish and Bland walked along the corridor together, Bland picking up his document folder from a hall table. Opposite the door to room 204 stood Freddy and Silas, both wearing suits and ties. When Hamish and Bland went to open the room door, both Freddy and Silas donned sunglasses and stood with their hands clasped in front of them, as though on guard.

Room 204 was an extremely comfortable bedroom, with enough space for a sofa, armchair and coffee table in an area near the large window. The curtains were drawn and the lights were on. What was not immediately obvious was that the windows were covered on the outside and locked on the inside. No one could see in or out. The bigger of the two men sat in the armchair, handcuffs on his wrists. He looked up when they entered, seeing the policeman, the American and, outside in the corridor, two guards. Without being too obvious, Bland made sure the man had noticed Freddy and Silas, then closed the door.

"Those guys are there for your protection," he said, smiling. "We don't want any of your old buddies paying you a visit, now, do we?"

"What 'buddies' would they be?" asked the man.

"Come on, let's not play games here," said Bland, he and Hamish seating themselves on the sofa. "You were one of what we have come to know as the Dozen. Did you go by the name of Smith or Martin—or maybe McAllister? Not that it matters, we know those are fake names."

"You are actually John Cox," Hamish said, holding up the driving license he had just taken from the man's wallet, having relieved the man of his wallet and phone before loading him into the car outside the Jacobite. "We know you've done time for assault and for housebreaking."

"Naturally, we have access to all of your official records," Bland said, "but what we'd like to know is how you originally got involved with the Dozen. You see, you come across as more of a common criminal than a professional spy. You're certainly no James Bond or Jason Bourne, are you?"

"I want to see a lawyer."

"Sure, you can see a lawyer. Did the boss recommend one you should contact? I'd advise you not to use that one. He'll be paid by the boss and reporting back to the boss on everything you say and do—and where you are."

"But I don't know where I am!" Cox yelled.

"Aye, and that way you can't blab it to anyone in the outside world you do eventually talk to," Hamish said. "We want to keep you safe, John. You know how the boss operates. You know how his sort deal wi' folk they see as a threat."

"This is bollocks," Cox spat. "You can't keep me here. You haven't even arrested me."

"I can arrest you, if you like," Hamish said, pouting his lip and spreading his hands. "I can do you for attempted murder, but as soon as I do that, I have to feed you into the system for processing. You'll have to leave here, go to a normal police station, and I'm guessing the boss will find you in no time at all."

"Have a think about it," Bland said, standing to leave. "We don't know everything we want to about the Dozen just yet. You help us put some of the pieces together, and we can help you stay alive."

Hamish and Bland left the room and Silas stepped forward, making a show of locking the door.

"He thinks he's tough," Bland said, "but we can break him eventually."

"We don't have until eventually," Hamish said. "We can't keep up this pretense forever, and the one they call the boss will realize they're missing soon enough. When that happens, he'll be in the wind. We'll never find him."

"True," Bland said, "but I get the impression Cox's buddy's not going to be quite such a tough nut to crack. Let's have a word with him."

"His real name is Brian Petrie," Hamish said, perusing the man's driving license. "Daviot sent me everything they have on him, just like wi' Cox."

When they opened the door to room 203, Petrie was treated to the same view of the "security guards" as Cox had, with the added bonus of a uniformed army colonel being handed a folder by a smart female aide as they walked past the door. As far as Petrie was concerned, this "safe house" he had been brought to was a very busy facility.

Room 203 was only slightly different to 204, on the opposite side of the corridor. The main difference was the view but, as the windows were also temporarily non-functional, there was virtually no difference at all. Petrie sat in the armchair, in handcuffs, looking utterly terrified.

"Mr. Petrie," Hamish said, he and Bland seating themselves on the sofa. "Brian…" He made a pretense of flicking through the folder he had carried in. "You've been a bit of a bad lad in the past, have you no', Brian? Shoplifting, burglary, car theft… nothing as bad as murder and attempted murder, though. It's all got a bit out o' hand has it no'? Things have spun right out o' control, eh?"

Petrie nodded, but said nothing.

"Your buddy Cox tells us that all he did was drive the car," Bland lied. "Kenny Robb told us that all he did was act as lookout. They both fingered you for the murder of Callum Graham and the attempted murder of Dennis McGill. You're in a whole heap of trouble, Brian."

"It wasn't me!" Petrie wailed. "I didn't do those things. What they did made me sick to the stomach. They made me help them!"

"Who did, Brian?" Hamish asked.

"John and the boss," said Petrie. "I don't understand why those people had to die."

"Those people?" Hamish asked. "Graham died, Brian, but we got to McGill in the nick of time. He's alive and well. You saw him."

"I didn't mean him," Petrie said, quietly. "I meant that poor bugger down in Glasgow."

"Edward Chalmers," Bland said. "You burned him alive."

"No, no' me! No' John, either. We don't know Glasgow, so the boss got somebody else to do that. He knows folk down there. He knows folk all over. He knows all sorts o' stuff. That's how he stays one step ahead o' the police."

"You were only one very short step ahead o' us at Dennis McGill's cottage," Hamish pointed out. "I have dash-cam footage o' a silver Audi speeding from the scene. Is that your car?"

"No' my car," Petrie said. "Yon's the boss's motor."

"How did you get tangled up in all this?" Bland asked. "Were you like Kenny? Were you recruited through the peace camp?"

"I was never at any peace camp," Petrie scoffed. "John and I did time together. We shared a cell, became pals. When we got out, he got a message offerin' us work. Nothing too difficult at first, just drivin' or breakin' in somewhere to steal whatever it was the boss wanted."

"The boss recruited you straight out of the jail?" Hamish said.

"Aye," Petrie confirmed. "We were both hard up and it was easy money."

"Did you no' realize that he was running a network o' spies and you were helping him do it?" Hamish asked.

"At the time, we didn't care that much. As time goes by, though, you get to thinkin' more about that sort o' stuff, don't you?"

"You'll have plenty of time to think about that when we get you to the States, my friend," Bland said. "A lifetime, I reckon."

"I don't want to go!" Petrie pleaded with them. "Can I no' just bide here?"

"Do jail time here?" Bland said. "How long do you think you'd live before the boss caught up with you?"

There was a knock at the door and a woman wearing a blue, fitted dress walked in. Hamish stared in horror—it was Elspeth! What was she doing? She would ruin everything, just as they were starting to get Petrie talking!

"Just in from Langley, sir," Elspeth said, in a perfect Midwestern American accent, handing Bland a file.

"Thank you, Miss Grant," Bland said, sparing Elspeth barely a glance. She left the room while he browsed the file. Then he stood and motioned Hamish to follow him. "We got another lead. Maybe we don't need these bozos."

They left the room, Silas locking the door and Hamish rounding on Elspeth, who was standing in the corridor.

"What are you doing?" he hissed, keeping his voice low lest Cox or Petrie should hear.

"Playing a part," Elspeth said, smiling and moving to stand by the uniformed colonel and Priscilla. "Ironic, isn't it? This could be the biggest story of my career, but I may never be able to report any of it, so I may as well be in it."

"We don't have time for idle chat, Hamish," Bland said, handing Elspeth's folder, full of blank sheets of paper, back to her. "Cox is going to give us nothing at this point, but Petrie is singing. We need to press him on the boss and find out who he is."

"If he actually knows," Hamish said. "Let's work up to that by getting him to talk about the way they worked together— his version of Moira's dead letter drops."

They walked back into the room, seating themselves on the sofa.

"So you were recruited when you came out of prison, Brian," Bland said. "How did the boss contact you when he had work for you?"

"He would phone John and tell us where to meet him," Petrie said. "It was ay away out in the wilds. We would drive in John's car to wherever the boss had left his car. He said that was to make sure nobody was followin' us. Then we ay used his car, lately yon silver Audi. One o' us would drive and he sat in the back, hunched down so that no one could see him. I don't know why he bothered wi' that. He ay knew the best route to take to avoid accidents or holdups. He ay knew where any police patrols would be. Nobody that mattered was ever goin' to see him."

"You saw him, though, Brian," Bland pointed out. "What does he look like? Is he tall, short, young, old..."

"He's certainly no' young," Petrie said. "Taller than me and broader. No' much hair left on top, but a bit o' a beard."

"Did he talk much when you were driving him?" Hamish asked.

"Apart from tellin' us what we had to do, he never said a word. He just sat hunched in his seat eatin' chocolate shortie."

Hamish sat up straight and shot a glance at Bland, who immediately realized something was up.

"We're going to take a break now, Brian," Bland said, standing once again. "One of our guys will bring you some tea."

They left the room and Hamish leaned against the wall in the hallway, breathing hard.

"It's Lachlan," Hamish said. "Lachlan is the boss, the head o' the network."

"Just because he eats chocolate cookies?" Bland said, doubtfully.

"No," Hamish replied. "It's no' just that. Blair said that Chalmers's murder in Glasgow was ordered by a man in the north. Lochcarron is way north o' Glasgow. Then look at the way Cox and Petrie were recruited—a cop would know their records and how to trace them as soon as they were out o' the jail.

"They're ay saying that the boss knows things, even where police cars might be—Lachlan would be able to find out that sort o' thing. He would know how to stay one step ahead o' the police. He would know how to find a couple o' heavies in Glasgow. And then there's the way he spoke to me, almost desperate to know about Jean Graham and the McGills. You mind o' what Graham told his niece? 'Trust no one—especially the police.'"

"I guess he fits the description, too, but there's a real easy way to rule him out, Hamish," Bland said.

"Aye," Hamish agreed, picking his phone from his pocket. "I don't want to believe its Lachlan, but Daviot can send me photos from his file."

Without asking why Hamish might want photos of a police officer in Lochcarron, Superintendent Daviot sent them straight to Hamish's phone within five minutes. Hamish and Bland walked into the room behind Freddy, who was delivering a tea tray, still wearing dark glasses.

"We need you to look at something for us, Brian," Bland said, and Hamish held his phone in front of Petrie's face, a head shot of Lachlan on the screen. Petrie blanched.

"The boss…"

Hamish and Bland left the room.

"What do we do now?" Bland asked.

"Daviot can get officers to Lochcarron fast," Hamish said, already thumbing the superintendent's number on his phone. "They'll pick him up if he's still there. Daviot can also get cars on the road looking for the Audi and every cop in Scotland looking for Lachlan."

"What about these two?" Bland asked, cocking thumbs at rooms 203 and 204.

"They're murderers," Hamish said. "We'll hold them in the cell at Lochdubh until they can be taken to Strathbane."

Daviot immediately issued an alert for all officers to be on the lookout for Sergeant Lachlan Doig, and made sure that he'd be picked up the moment he went near any port, airport or railway station, but Hamish wasn't finished yet. He made half a dozen calls to friends scattered across Sutherland, asking them to keep their eyes peeled for Lachlan's Audi. Within a few minutes, he had a return call from Dougie Tennant, a mechanic who ran a filling station on the Scourie road.

"Your Audi just came past here like a bat out o' hell, Hamish," he said, "heading north."

"Thanks, Dougie," Hamish said. "If he comes back, promise me you'll stay out o' his way. I don't want you, or anyone else, tangling wi' this devil."

Dougie promised, and Hamish called another number, he and Bland already making their way to the Land Rover.

"It's Hamish Macbeth here, Moira," he said, when Moira Stephenson answered. "We've found out who the boss is, and he's headed north in a silver Audi. We know he went past Scourie. If he comes your way, hide and pretend you're no' home, but call me. Don't let him in, even if he's dressed like a police officer. We're heading up your way now."

With Hamish at the wheel, blue lights flashing and siren wailing whenever they encountered another vehicle, they made good time on the road to Cromish. Bland put in a call to Moira when they were close, but she had seen nothing of Lachlan.

"If he planned on using Moira to help him, he'd have reached her by now," Hamish reasoned. "If he's carried on north past Cromish—"

Cutting through the noise of the car surging along the road at high speed came the sound of his phone ringing. He pressed a button to let the car's system answer the call.

"Crivens, Hamish, it sounds like you're on the road again," came Lachlan's voice. "I'd have thought you'd have had enough of that lately."

"Lachlan, where are you?" Hamish asked. "We need to sit down and talk."

"The time for talking is past, I'm afraid," Lachlan answered. "I have nothing I want to say to you except don't waste your time looking for me. By tonight I'll be long gone and you'll never find me."

"How could you do this, Lachlan?" Hamish pleaded, struggling to understand how someone he thought he had known for years could turn out to be a complete stranger. "How could you turn against your own folk?"

"Ha! Don't be daft, laddie!" Lachlan's mocking laugh sounded almost sympathetic. "The likes o' you were never my folk. I've been living a lie in this country since afore you were born. I seem like one o' you, I sound like one o' you, but you can ask your American friend how much that really means. I'm no' one o' you and now I'm done. Almost all my team's gone, so leave me be, now, laddie—the game's over."

He hung up and Hamish flicked a glance at Bland.

"What was he talking about?" he asked. "What did he mean about 'living a lie'? He's a police officer! I've known him since I started in the job!"

"You've known who he said he was," Bland said, shaking his head. "You've known who everybody believed he was. From what he said, I reckon he must have been infiltrated into this country by the Russians as a young man. He'll have had all the right paperwork and support to back up a phony identity when he joined the police and, once he was in, it was just a case of biding his time, working away year after year until he could start recruiting his network."

"He said, 'Almost all my team's gone,'" Hamish reasoned. "Of the Dozen, the only two he could turn to for help are Moira Stephenson and Kenneth Robb. Moira didn't know him, and he'd never met her. I'm pretty sure she would have told us if he'd showed up at her place. If he needed help when the chips were down, he'd turn to somebody he knew, somebody he could trust."

"That means Kenneth Robb," Bland said, "and if he's heading north past Cromish, he's on the road to Durness."

"And Robb has a boat—that could be part of his escape plan."

By the time they reached Durness, Hamish having pushed the car hard, covering the road in less time than even he would have thought possible, it was early evening and the bright light of the late summer day was starting to fade. The pier at Keoldale was closer than Robb's cottage, so they headed there first to check on the boat.

A small crowd was gathered near the landing stage. A few locals were looking out across the water and a clutch of curious tourists with mountain bikes had joined them to see what was attracting so much attention.

"What's going on?" Hamish asked a local man, who shook his head in disbelief, pointing out across the water, shading his eyes from the glare with his other hand against the peak of his tweed cap.

"Kenny Robb's took his boat out," the man explained. "He's took a man across to the landing stage on the other side…madness…"

"What do you mean?" asked Bland.

"Only the ferry should be making that trip," the man said,

indicating a small boat moored at the pier, where two men in overalls were working on its engine. "It's being overhauled today because no one's allowed to cross to the Parph. There's live firing over at Cape Wrath today. The navy's been dropping shells in there all afternoon. Madness. They advertise these firing days well in advance. Kenny knows he shouldn't be out there."

They watched a small boat making its way back to the pier. Hamish grabbed a pair of binoculars from the Land Rover.

"That's Robb in the boat all right," he confirmed, "and I can see Lachlan on the other side."

"Why would he want to go across there?" Bland asked.

"There are isolated bays and beaches on the coast where a bigger boat than Robb's would be able to come in and pick him up without anyone knowing," Hamish explained, "and he'll be counting on no one following him into the firing area."

"Won't it all be cordoned off?" Bland asked, borrowing the binoculars.

"There are no real fences," Hamish said. "There are checkpoints on the main paths into Cape Wrath, but Lachlan's canny enough to avoid those."

"He's got in a blue van, and it's moving up a track from the landing stage!" Bland said.

"He's stolen the tourist minibus," Hamish said. "That's the only vehicle over there. It travels the track up to the lighthouse about ten miles away."

"I've got to get after him," Bland said, hurrying onto the pier as soon as Robb's boat pulled in. "Hey you! I need your boat to take me across!"

"I'm no' making that trip again," Robb said sourly.

"I don't need you, buddy," Bland said, pushing him aside, "just your boat!"

He climbed aboard, studying the outboard motor and deciding he was familiar enough with the type before starting it up and calling to Hamish.

"You can't come with me, Hamish. It's too risky. That guy's my man and I…"

He looked up to see Hamish on the pier. Robb was in handcuffs, one hand either side of a lamppost, and Hamish was holding two mountain bikes.

"We'll need these on the other side to catch up wi' Lachlan," was all he said, passing the first bike to Bland.

"Stick to the deep-water channel," the man in the tweed cap advised, pointing out the snaking route across to the Parph, "otherwise you can easy get stuck on a sandbank. I'll phone to try to get the firing stopped, but it might take a wee while."

The journey across the Kyle of Durness took only ten minutes, then they were on the mountain bikes, pedaling up the track, the bikes better suited to the rough going than the minibus. A few minutes later, they came across the bus, abandoned in a ditch, and spotted a solitary figure on the hillside in the distance, hurrying along a rabbit track.

"That's him!" Bland cried, dismounting. "Come on, Hamish, we can catch up with him in no time!"

Leaving the bikes by the minibus, they set a fast pace up the hill, although it still took almost half an hour to close in on their quarry, by which time they were traversing high moorland that was pockmarked with craters and the occasional wreck of an old military vehicle that had been used for target practice. They had heard only one explosion, echoing round the hills like distant thunder, since they had begun their chase and, just as Hamish predicted, Lachlan had taken a route that avoided any military checkpoints.

"Lachlan!" he shouted to his old friend, now no more than two hundred meters away. "Give it up, man! You'll never get away now!"

Lachlan looked round at his pursuers, paused for a second, then dodged behind the wall of a ruined bothy.

"We've got him now, Hamish!" yelled Bland, pressing on.

Suddenly, Hamish felt a numbing sensation and a bright light filled his head. He fell to his knees in a dip in the ground.

"James," he groaned, and Bland rushed to his aid.

"What is it?" Bland asked. "What's wrong?"

Looking up, Hamish was astonished to see a shimmering figure at Bland's side, and heard a soft voice, growing louder, repeating over and over: "Hamish! No!" It was Elspeth's voice. He reached up, grabbed hold of Bland and dragged him to the ground.

The air was suddenly filled with a momentary sound like a zip fastener being swiftly drawn, and there was a searing flash of light and heat immediately followed by the roar of a massive explosion. They hugged the damp ground in their hollow, debris and stone fragments flying overhead. When all was still once more, they could hear the echoes of the explosion drifting off into the distance and Hamish opened his eyes.

A cloud of smoke hung in the air, billowing upward from a crater where the ruined bothy once stood. There was no trace of Lachlan. Bland stood, staring at the charred hole in the ground.

"I would have been in there," he said, stunned, "with Lachlan."

"Aye," Hamish said slowly, "and me at your side."

The two men turned and walked slowly back to the track where they had abandoned the mountain bikes.

The population of Durness doubled with the number of police officers and vehicles that flooded onto the peninsula over the following couple of hours.

Hamish was amazed. He patrolled vast swathes of Sutherland alone all year round, come rain, snow or sun. Now, when the danger and excitement were over, there were more police than you could shake a truncheon at.

An incident center was set up at Durness Village Hall, a modern building next to the John Lennon Memorial Garden, and Hamish began the wearisome process of answering questions and filling out forms. Superintendent Daviot arrived after a couple of hours, in a show of support for which Hamish was grateful, if surprised. Only when the TV crews arrived, Elspeth among them, and the superintendent took his place in front of the cameras, did Hamish realize that Daviot had an ulterior motive for his presence.

Bland was noticeably reluctant to answer any questions or participate in any formal interviews. Then came the sound of a powerful helicopter flying low over the village, making for the military landing pad at Faraid Head. Bland turned to Hamish.

"Sounds like my ride home just arrived," he said, smiling.

"You're leaving?" Hamish said. "Just like that?"

"My people will want me to talk them through everything that's happened without all of this...fuss and publicity," he said.

"What about the Dozen?" Hamish asked. "Or the four of them who are left?"

"Robb, Cox and Petrie will get a proper grilling from your guys and ours, I should think. Then, they'll face whatever charges your people want to bring against them—including murder."

"And Moira Stephenson?"

"As she said herself," Bland said with a grin, "she's small fry. I'll put in a good word for her and, if you do the same, maybe they'll just leave the poor old woman alone."

They shook hands awkwardly before Bland laughed and wrapped Hamish in a bear hug.

"You know," he said, "I love your part of Scotland. Don't be surprised if I show up here again on vacation."

"Don't do that without letting me know," Hamish said. "I'll take you for a dander in the hills and show you the most beautiful country in the world."

"I won't forget what you did back there at Cape Wrath," Bland said, a more serious look on his face. "I reckon we're quits now, buddy."

"Good." Hamish smiled. "There should be no debts between friends."

Bland was then hustled out of the building by two Americans in suits, whom he clearly knew well, and Elspeth found a moment to catch Hamish alone.

"Are you all right?" she asked.

"Never better," he answered, yawning. "A bit tired, but glad to be done wi' this whole sorry business."

Over a cup of coffee in a quiet corner, he ran through the whole story of everything that had happened, as promised, and she swore that she would never broadcast a full report.

"It was close," she said, finally. "I felt it."

"I don't know what—"

"Aye, but you do," she said, smiling. She leant forward and kissed his cheek. "We're never really that far apart, you and I, Hamish Macbeth."

He was summoned into another meeting before being taken to Strathbane where a long night of questions and storytelling stretched ahead of him.

The following evening, Hamish sat at his favorite spot in the Napoli, with Willie fussing around the table and Claire sitting opposite, wearing the dress she had worn for the date he forgot. They sampled a couple of glasses of the Valpolicella and chatted through a starter, which surprised Willie as he'd never known Hamish to order anything other than pasta with meatballs. He was almost relieved when Hamish then ordered exactly that for his main course. Claire was hugely impressed with Lucia's cooking.

"I've been to Italy on holiday a couple of times," she said, tucking into a creamy linguini with Moray Firth langoustines, "but I've never tasted anything as delicious as this and..."

She looked across the table to see Hamish sitting back in his chair, his chin on his chest, sound asleep.

When he woke a few minutes later, having heard something that sounded like the slamming of the restaurant door, the seat opposite him was empty. Claire had gone. He was tucked up in his chair, a crisp, clean tablecloth wrapped around him. Struggling out of the improvised blanket, he spotted a note scribbled on a paper napkin by his plate. It said: "Because you fell asleep, this doesn't count as a date. Unless you get your act together, by the time you next see him, you'll owe Mike £50!"

"Willie!" he called, but Willie was already there, whisking the tablecloth off Hamish with a flourish and folding it neatly. He then sat down in Claire's place, pouring each of them another glass of wine.

"You know, Hamish," he said as they clinked glasses. "I think yon Claire's a grand lass. She said you'd had a hard time ower the past few days and we should let you sleep. She's properly condensatorate. I'd even go so far as to say altruistic."

"Well, Willie…" Hamish said, thinking about the note, then realizing what Willie had just said, "…hold on a wee minute…I haven't the faintest idea what condensatorate might mean, but altruistic is exactly the right word."

"Aye, I ken fine," Willie said, holding up his phone. "I Googled it while you were snoring. The thing is, Hamish, we've all seen the two o' you together and we've no' seen you look so happy in a long while. She's a wee belter, but if you keep taking the lassie for granted she'll melt through your fingers and disappear like spring snow."

"Willie," Hamish said, his rusty eyebrows shooting up toward his hairline, "that's no' only the right words, it's even quite poetic."

"Aye," Willie agreed, nodding, "I heard something like it in a song on the radio in the kitchen just now. What I really mean is, you need to do something, or you'll lose her."

"Flowers, Hamish!" Lucia popped her head round the kitchen door. "Send her a big bunch o' flowers first thing tomorrow!"

"Flowers…" Hamish considered the notion for a second, then nodded for fear of being caught contemplating the expense. "Thank you, Lucia. Flowers is a braw idea, and you're right again, Willie," he added, slapping a hand on the table and taking a slug of wine. "I need to make it up to her. I know Claire's schedule, and she's no' working tomorrow night, so book this table for us."

"Sorry, but it's too late for that, Hamish," Willie said.

"Too late…" Hamish said softly, the weight of a forlorn expression seeming to hang so heavy on his features that he leant forward, resting his elbows on the table.

"Aye," Willie said, grinning, "Claire's already booked this table for the two o' you tomorrow!"

Hamish scowled at Willie, then looked up to see Lucia joining them at the table. He smiled, then laughed and poured a glass of wine for her.

"Here's to Claire," he said, and they touched glasses. "There will be flowers in the morn, and a fine evening to follow. Wi' a lass like Claire and friends like you here in Lochdubh, I've not a doubt in my head that I'm the luckiest man alive!"

About the Authors

M. C. Beaton, hailed as the "Queen of Crime" by the *Globe and Mail,* was the author of the *New York Times* and *USA Today* bestselling Agatha Raisin novels—the basis for the hit series on Acorn TV and public television—as well as the Hamish Macbeth series. Born in Scotland, Beaton started her career writing historical romances under several pseudonyms as well as her maiden name, Marion Chesney. Her books have sold more than 22 million copies worldwide.

A long-time friend of M. C. Beaton's, **R. W. Green** has written numerous works of fiction and nonfiction. He lives in Surrey with his family and a black Labrador called Flynn.